JN409661

눈사람 속의 검은 항아리

도서출판 아시아에서는《바이링궐 에디션 한국 대표 소설》을 기획하여 한국의 우수한 문학을 주제별로 엄선해 국내외 독자들에게 소개합니다. 이 기획은 국내외 우수한 번역가들이 참여하여 원작의 품격을 최대한 살렸습니다. 문학을 통해 아시아의 정체성과 가치를 살피는 데 주력해 온 도서출판 아시아는 한국인의 삶을 넓고 깊게 이해하는 데 이 기획이 기여하기를 기대합니다.

Asia Publishers presents some of the very best modern Korean literature to readers worldwide through its new Korean literature series 〈Bilingual Edition Modern Korean Literature〉. We are proud and happy to offer it in the most authoritative translation by renowned translators of Korean literature. We hope that this series helps to build solid bridges between citizens of the world and Koreans through a rich in-depth understanding of Korea.

바이링궐 에디션 한국 대표 소설 031
Bi-lingual Edition Modern Korean Literature 031

The Dark Jar within the Snowman

김소진

눈사람 속의 검은 항아리

Kim So-jin

ASIA
PUBLISHERS

Contents

눈사람 속의 검은 항아리

The Dark Jar within the Snowman

내가 겸사겸사 미아리 셋집엘 한번 다녀오겠다는 말을 꺼내자 이번에는 어머니가 펄쩍 뛰었다. 그깟 돈 삼만 원 은행 온라인으로 부쳐버리면 그만 아니냐는 거였다.

"그 집 남자가 요즘은 문짝 샤씨 달러 다니는 모양이더라. 낮에 가봤자 코빼기도 구경하기 어려워서. 그 예전에 요한네 집에 세 살던 오종종한 해자 엄마 있지? 웃음이 헤퍼서 남자한테 그저 얻어맞고 살던 그 여자 얼굴을 꼭 닮은 그 집 여편네도 뭘 하러 쏘다니는지 갈 때마다 아이들만 둘이서 집을 지키고 있더라구."

"그 집 전화번호 있어요?"

"저기 가방 찾아보면 나오긴 나올 텐데. 늙은이 혼자

When I mentioned I would drop by the rental house in Miari for this and that, Mother would have none of it. She said I could just as easily wire the thirty thousand *won* through the bank.

"I hear he is going around putting in door frames these days. You won't catch so much as a glimpse of him if you go there during the day. You know Hae-ja's mom, who had a face with small features and roomed at Yo-han's way back when? Remember how she'd get beat up by her man because she'd smile at anyone and everyone? The woman at the Miari house has a face just like hers. I have no idea what she does all day long, but whenever I

있는 듯하니깐 아주 만만히 보고 능갈을 치는 데 이골이 났더라구. 두 젊은 양주가 안팎으로 말이야. 여깄다. 구, 일, 사에…… 아유 칩칩해."

삼만 원은 입동 무렵에 연탄에서 기름형으로 바꿔 설치한 셋집 보일러가 기습 한파에 얼었다며 손을 보려 하니 보내달라고 셋집 사내가 기별한 것이었다.

"이 추위에 보일러가 아예 서버렸대요?"

"그런 건 아니고 온수통이 얼어서 따신 물을 못 받아서 쓴다는데 원. 지 입으로도 그러더구먼. 보일러 놓을 때 보니 그 온수통께가 허전해서 온 사람들한테 뭘로 좀 덮어야 하는 거 아니냐구 했다는 거야. 근데 요즘 같은 세상에 일 더하기 좋아하는 이가 어딨니? 그러니깐 그 사람들이 아이구 그냥 괜찮다고 그러면서 쓱싹 바르고 시브저기 가더니 그 동티가 났다는 거지 뭐. 자기도 남의 집 문짝서껀 주무르러 다니는 사람이면 눈썰미가 있어서 그런 것쯤은 기술자들이 안 해줘도 스스로 알아서 재활용도 안 되는 그 흔한 누더기 짜배기라도 덮어놔야지 그게 뭐야. 자기 집 아니라고 데면데면하고서는 그것 얼어붙어 따신 물 안 나온다고 돈타령이야, 돈타령을? 내가 자기한테 한 달에 기껏 돈 십만 원 셋값 받

go there, it's just the two kids watching the house."

"Do you have their phone number?"

"It should be somewhere in that bag. They must think I'm this old patsy who's all by herself so I'd be easy to fool. Both the man and the woman. Oh, here it is. Nine-one-four...oh I can't see too well."

The thirty thousand *won* was what the guy tenant had said he needed, because the oil boiler at the rental property, the one we had installed in early November to replace the briquette burner, had frozen in the cold snap and needed to be fixed.

"The boiler's stopped working in this cold?"

"No, no, just the hot water tank is frozen so they can't get hot water. He said himself that when they were putting in the boiler it looked exposed so he asked the workers if they shouldn't cover it with something. But these days, who wants to do more work than he has to? So they said it'd be fine, finished up the plastering just like that and took off. And now this mess. I mean, even without a technician coming, if you make a living handling other people's doors, you should have enough of a clue to be able to put a piece of rag around it, the kind you can't even recycle. But because it's not your own house, you don't care about it and now that it's

아서 어느 구녕에 처바르는지 다 알면서 말이야. 지난 달엔 재개발됩네 하니깐 이젠 관에서도 달라붙어서 토지세 내라 무슨 세 내라 하면서 거진 돈 삼백이 다 깨지게 생겼는데 말이야. 아주 낯이 맨질맨질한 사람들이야 생각할수록."

이 년 반 전에 성남 근처에서 일 년 계약으로 살던 신혼살림을 접어서 신도시에 들어갈 때, 미아리 집에서 혼자 살던 어머니를 모셔왔다. 말이 모셔온 거지 집사람이 다시 직장에 나가기 위해선 아이를 봐줄 사람이 절실했다. 그 때문에 어머니는 뭔가 서운한 일이 있으면 동냥자루 타령을 하였다. 몸도 시원찮은데 애를 보자니 차라리 밥을 빌어먹는 한이 있더라도 혼자 나가서 사시겠다고 까탈 아닌 까탈을 부리곤 하였다. 어머니가 그렇게 큰소리를 낼 수 있는 배경에는 물론 그 세내준 미아리 집이 있었다. 우리가 아니래도 당신 몸 하나 거처시킬 공간은 있다고 은근히 내비치는 태였다.

"더군다나 그 보일러가 완전 새것으로 해단 건데 왜 그리 고장이 쉬 난단 말이야. 얼마나 시덥잖게 다루며 썼으면 몇 달도 채 안 돼 그 지경이 됐을라구."

처음에 셋집에서 겨울을 날 기름보일러를 달아달라

frozen with no hot water you keep carrying on asking for money? When he knows only too well what I do with the dammed hundred thousand *won* of rent I get from him. And since the news of re-development hit last month, the government has gotten involved, saying I need to pay property tax-es and whatnot, so I'm almost out three mil, you know. The more I think about it, the more I realize how thick-skinned they are."

We started to live with and care for Mother two and half years ago when we moved to a newly de-veloped city after a year as newlyweds in a rental near Seongnam. She had been living by herself in the old Miari house. I say care for, but in reality we were in desperate need of a babysitter so that my wife could go back to work. Because of that, whenever Mother felt slighted she would bring up the panhandler's bag. She would kind of grumble, saying she'd rather go out and live by herself, even if that meant she had to beg for food. She'd rather do that than be in poor health and watch the kid. Beneath that threat was, of course, that Miari rental property. Even if we didn't care for her, she had a place to go.

"And that boiler was brand new when we put it

는 연락이 왔을 때 어머니는 중고품을 하나 헐값에 달 요량이었다. 재개발을 앞둔 그 동네도 길어야 일 년 안에 철거가 시작될 기세여서 일 년 쓰고 버릴 것을 굳이 돈 더 얹어주며 새것으로 할 게 뭐 있냐는 생각이었다. 그래서 셋집 여자한테 알아서 중고를 하나 골라보라고 했더니 사십만 원 견적이 나왔다고 알려왔다. 그러자 아버지 살아 계실 적부터 친하게 지내온 석유집의 임씨 아저씨한테 전화를 걸어 시세를 알아본 어머니는 혀를 내둘렀다.

"새것으로 해도 사십오만 원이면 뒤집어쓰고 남는다는데 뭔 말라빠진 중고가 사십만 원씩이야 응? 이놈의 집이 아주 작정을 해도 단단히 한 모양이야. 구 경계선인 한길 너머 미아동 쪽으로는 거진 철거가 끝나서 집집마다 헌 보일러가 남아돌아 너도나도 갖다 쓰라고 난리들이라고 그러더구먼."

"품삯이 많이 들잖을까요?"

"삯이 들어도 그렇지, 그놈의 집이 자기네한테 먼 인척이 되어 잘 아는 물역 가게에서 들여 놓겠다 그러는데 그게 바로 아삼륙으로 붙어먹으려는 깜깜한 심보지 뭐야. 그래서 내가 임씨 영감한테 부탁을 해서 아예 새

in, so how does it break down so easily? How rough they must have treated it for it to be like that in just months!"

When the tenants first requested to have an oil boiler for the winter, Mother figured she would install a used one at a low cost. She reasoned there was no point in paying more for a new one, when it seemed it would be less than a year before demolition would start in that area. So she asked the female tenant to look into a used one, who reported that it would cost about four hundred thousand *won*. Mother then called and asked Mr. Yim, an oil vendor she'd known since before Father's passing, and was at a loss for words afterward.

"He says four hundred fifty should more than cover a new unit, so why are they talking four hundred for a damned used one, huh? They must be bent on getting me, for sure. The houses near Mia-dong on the other side of the broad street, the old town limit, have almost all been taken down, so there are lots of used boilers lying around, they say, and people are asking others to come take them away."

"Don't you think the labor would cost too much?

"Even so. The tenants wanted to go through a

걸루다 달아달라고 했어. 괜히 중고로 달면 뭐가 어쨌네 저쨌네 뒷말이 많이 나올 집구석이고 그러면 내가 이 시큰시큰한 종짓굽을 이끌고 그때마다 어떻게 달려가겠니? 생각 같아서는 다시 벼룩시장에다 한 줄 싣고 싶지만 또다시 몇 번 발걸음하고 도배해줄 생각을 하니 입맛이 써서 원."

"기왕 말 나온 김에 제가 한번 다녀와 본다니까요."

"거긴 뭐 허러?"

"창이 형 만나서 이런저런 얘기도 들어두면 좋잖아요. 그리고 셋집 연탄광 쪽에 달아낸 작은방에서 가져올 것도 있구요."

"뭘?"

"영정으로 썼던 아버지 사진틀도 솜이불 보따리 틈새에 아직 박혀 있을 텐데……"

"그 생각은 잊고 꿈에도 하지 마라. 그 뱀의 허물 뒤집어쓴 것처럼 아물아물한 사진은 가져다 어디다 두려고? 애어멈이 그 형상을 보면 얼씨구나 하겠구나!"

말은 그렇게 했지만 어머니도 짐짓 내가 한번 재개발을 앞둔 그 동네를 후딱 살피고 왔으면 하는 눈치였다. 서너 달 전에 본격적으로 재개발 승인이 떨어지자 그곳

building materials seller who's a distant relative of theirs. Like I wouldn't know what they were trying to pull, getting in cahoots with each other. So I asked Old Man Yim to go put in a new unit. God forbid if I gave them a used one, they'd never stop griping about this and that, and how could I run over there every time, with my bad knees and all? I'd just as well put in another ad for rent in the local circular but I get a bad taste in my mouth just thinking about having to go back and forth several times and putting up the wallpaper again."

"That's why I'm saying I'll go check it out while we're at it."

"What for?"

"It'd be good to see Chang and get caught up on the news. And there's some stuff I need to get from that little room we added on to the briquette storage room at the house."

"What is it?"

"Well, the framed photo we used for Father's funeral must still be there, wedged between the thick cotton comforter piles."

"Oh, don't even think about it. What are you gonna do with that fuzzy photo that looks like it's covered in snake slough? Your wife would be so ex-

분위기가 급격히 달라졌다. 심지어는 현대부동산인가 하는 데서 어머니 앞으로도 딱지를 넘길 의향이 없느냐는 제안이 들어와 '넉 장'을 받고 매매를 하기로 전화로 약속까지 했다가 내가 말리는 바람에 취소한 적도 있었다. 마침 임씨 아저씨 아들인 창이 형이 재개발조합에서 간사 자리를 꿰차고 있다는 말을 들은 어머니는, 내가 평소 가까이 지내온 창이 형을 만나면 그곳 분위기나 시세에 대한 정확한 정보를 얻어듣고 오지 않을까 내심 짐작하는 모양이었다.

경의선 기차를 타고 나와 신촌에서 미아리행 버스에 몸을 실었다. 광화문 네거리를 지나면서 차창 밖으로 펼쳐지는 풍경이 익숙해지면 질수록 내 머릿속에는 그날 새벽의 모습이 좀더 선명히 어른거리기 시작했다. 혹시 그 종이처럼 얇은 기억이 나를 이렇게 사라져 가려는 동네로 밀고 가는 것이 아닐까? 정말 그런지도 모를 일이었다. 창이 형을 만나 재개발 정보를 듣거나, 아버지 영정을 다시 꺼내오거나, 잇속 바른 셋집 사내를 만나 삼만 원을 직접 건네주며 다독거려주려고 나선다는 것은 어쩌면 허울뿐이지 않을까. 나는 머리통에 난혹을 더듬는 기분으로 손끝으로 옆머리를 짚으며 기억

cited to see that mug!"

So she said. But Mother still seemed to want me to go take a quick look around that neighborhood. After they got permission for redevelopment several months before, the air of that town changed immediately. Mother even fielded an offer from a Hyundae Realty to hand over her deed. She'd gotten as far as agreeing on four "big ones" over the phone before I talked her out of it. It seemed she'd figured, after learning that Chang, Mr. Yim's son, had gotten himself a position at the redevelopment association, that I might come away with insider information on the mood and the market if I saw him in person, since we'd always been close.

I got out to Sinchon on the Kyeong-ui Railway, then boarded a bus headed for Miari. The more familiar the scenery outside the window became as the bus passed the Gwanghwamun intersection, the more vivid the image of that dawn grew in my mind. Could that paper-thin memory now be driving me toward that fading town? That could have very well been the case. Perhaps getting information from Chang, retrieving Father's funeral photo, or placating that calculating tenant by handing over the thirty thousand *won* were only excuses. Feeling

의 끈질김에 대해 새삼 진저리치지 않을 수 없었다. 따져보니 이십 년도 더 바랜 기억이었다. 물론 지금 내가 가고자 하는 미아리 셋집에 대한 기억이 아니라 그 전에 국민학교 시절을 보낸 한 지붕 아홉 가구의 장석조네 집에 대한 기억이었다.

아마 설을 쇤 지 며칠 지나지 않은 때였을 것이다. 양말을 신은 채 부뚜막에 올라서 까치발을 하고 찬장 위에 얹어진 소쿠리 안을 휘저으면 아직도 뻣뻣하게 굳긴 했지만 부침개 쪼가리나 쉰 두부전 같은 게 손끝에 걸리곤 했다. 내가 태어나자 큰외숙모가 엄마의 산후조리를 봐주기 위해 마른 미역을 담아 갖고 올 때 쓴 것이라고 하니, 이미 십 년은 지난 그 소쿠리는 낡을 대로 낡아 테두리가 반쯤은 빠져나갔고 군데군데 풀어진 댓개비들이 날카롭게 비어져나와 자칫 맘이 급해 서둘다간 손톱 밑을 파고들거나 손등에 생채기를 내기 일쑤였다.

그 소쿠리를 더듬다가 찔린 가운데 손톱 밑의 감각이 아직 얼얼한데다 몇 해 전에 뇌졸중으로 쓰러지기까지 한 아버지가 그동안 입에 대지 않던 쇠고기 한 점을 배즙과 함께 삼켰다가 며칠째 자리보전을 하던 중이었으니 기껏해야 설에서 사나흘 이상은 벗어나지 않았을 것

as though I had bumps on my head, I massaged my temples with my fingertips as I shuddered at the tenacity of the memory. Come to think of it, it had been more than twenty years. Of course the memory was not about the rental property I was headed to now. It was about Jang Seok-jo's house, where I spent my childhood as part of one of the nine families who lived under one roof.

It must have been a few days into the lunar New Year. If you tippy-toed on the old-style cooking fireplace in the kitchen with your socks on and felt inside the wicker basket in the cupboard, your fingertips would catch things like leftover pieces of pancake and bits of old fried tofu, though they had gotten hard by then. My big aunt brought dried seaweed in the basket when she came over to look after my mother after she had just given birth to me. So the basket was over ten years old, and it looked its age: its rim was about half missing, and loose strands were sticking out sharply here and there, making it easy for you to get poked deep under your nails or get scratches on the back of your hand if you stuck your hand inside impatiently.

My middle finger was still smarting after stabbing it inside the basket, and my father, who had had a

이다. 어머니는 시큰한 나박김치 국물을 많이 먹으면 육식 때문에 덧이 난 아버지의 고혈압이 풀린다는 말을 어디서 듣고 왔는지 저녁이면 멕기칠이 벗겨진 양푼에 살얼음이 버석버석한 김칫국물을 담아 내왔다. 덕택에 며칠 간 기름 음식에 질린 내게 그 등골이 오싹하고 인중이 고무줄처럼 늘어나도록 차가운 나박김치 국물에 국수를 한 그릇 말아먹는 맛은 별미 중의 별미였다.

그런데 밤새 장을 빠져나와 오줌보로 슬금슬금 고여 든 김칫국물이 탈이었다. 평소 같으면 한밤중이나 새벽녘이나 가리지 않고 머리맡에 놓인 사기 요강에다 볼일을 보고 따순 공기가 다 빠져나가기 전에 다람쥐처럼 이부자리 속으로 되돌아오면 그만이었을 터였다. 하지만 설부터 정월 대보름까지 보름 동안은 요강을 쓸 수가 없었다. 어머니가 금했기 때문이었다. 어머니는 자신이 시집올 때 가져온 그 난초 무늬 사기 요강에 대해 엄청난 터부 의식을 갖고 있었다. 그것이 깨지거나 혹은 금이라도 가는 날이면 감당할 수 없는 커다란 동티가 생겨서 끔찍한 경우를 당할 것이라고 굳게 믿었다.

어머니가 전하는 얘기에 따르면 어렸을 적에 외할머니가 요강에 금이 간 것을 보고 걱정하시던 날 밤 소 장

stroke a few years before, was still bedridden from eating a piece of meat with pear juice for the first time in ages, so it could not have been more than several days since the New Year's. Someone must have told Mother the sour water of *nabak* kimchi was a good remedy for Father's high blood pressure, which the meat had worsened, because every evening she would bring out the kimchi water, slushy from the thin layer of ice on top, in a brass bowl with a worn-out plating. After days of greasy food, it was a real treat to have noodles dunked in that water, cold enough to give you shivers and make you tighten your upper lip.

But the problem with drinking that kimchi water was that it would escape my intestines and flood my bladder overnight. Whenever this happened, all I would have to do was go in the porcelain chamber pot behind my head and get back under the covers like a squirrel before all the warmth was lost. But we were not allowed to use the chamber pot for the two weeks between New Year's and the First Full Moon. Mother forbade us. She had a huge superstition about that porcelain chamber pot with orchid prints, the one that came with her when she married my father. She firmly believed that if it

사를 하시던 외할아버지가 실제로 뿔이 위아래로 어긋나게 솟은 검둥이 수소를 감쪽같이 도둑맞았다. 어머니의 외가 쪽으로 촌수를 따질 수 없을 만큼 멀어 그저 사돈이라고 부르는 한 집안에서는 평소 새살맞던 며느리가 정초에 요강을 부시러 나왔다가 깬 뒤로 배냇병신을 낳고 결국 집안도 몇 년 안에 풍비박산이 되었다는 것이다. 그런 요강이기에 특히나 정초부터 대보름까지는 각별히 조심하는 게 제일이고 그러자니 아예 화선지로 덮어 싸서 부엌 한구석에 모셔두고 쓰지 않는 게 상책이라고 엄마는 일러주었다.

나박김치 국물 때문에 눈을 떠보니, 아니 고개를 이불 밖으로 빼 창호지로 막은 봉창을 보니 아직 어스레한 새벽이었다. 사실은 진작에 깨서 이불 안에서 새우등을 한 채 꼼지락거리고 있었다. 어머니조차 깨어나지 않은 걸로 봐서 어지간히 이른 새벽이라는 걸 알고 있었다. 나는 겁이 많았다. 형을 깨울까 생각해봤지만 새벽잠에 유달리 약한 형이 순순히 내 부탁을 들어줄 리 만무했다. 그렇다고 누나를 깨우자니 알량한 자존심이 허락을 하지 않아 진땀을 흘리며 사타구니를 꽈배기처럼 꼬고 등뼈가 부러져라 구부러뜨렸다. 오줌이 몇 방울 질금거

broke or got cracked during that period, it would lead to something catastrophic.

According to her, when she was a little girl, on the very night her mother noticed a crack in their chamber pot, someone actually stole a black ox, the one with mismatching horns, from my grandfather, who sold cattle. On another part of her family, on a branch so far removed that she didn't even know how they were related to us, a careless daughter-in-law broke a chamber pot in the beginning of the year while washing it. Later, she gave birth to a retard and the family broke up within a few years. So, with urns, you'd best be extra careful for the couple of weeks following New Year's. And there was no better way to do that than to cover it with Chinese drawing paper and keep it out of the way in the corner of the kitchen, Mom said, and not use it.

When I opened my eyes, or rather, poked my head out from under the blanket, up early thanks to the *nabak* kimchi water, I saw through the paper-covered window that it was still gray out. Actually, I had been wide awake for a while, wiggling under the covers in the fetal position. I knew it had to be quite early in the morning, since even my

려 허벅지를 땃땃하게 적실 때쯤 해서 나는 욕을 바가지로 얻어먹으며 어머니를 깨울 것인가, 아니면 용감하게 혼자서 아홉 가구가 딸린 기찻집의 제일 끝자락에서 있는 변소로 갈 것인가 결정해야 했다. 나는 홀가분하게 후자를 택했다.

"어디 가니……"

"아, 아니요……"

"근데 우와기(윗도리의 일본말)는 왜 껴입고…… 부뚜막 옆 밥통에 미지근한 숭냉(숭늉) 있다."

문간 쪽에서 모로 누워 자던 엄마가 고개를 빼 뒤로 제치며 한마디 던지고는 다시 이불을 끌어당겼다. 엄마의 입에서 하얀 입김이 뿜어져 나왔다. 아마 내가 목이 말라서 일어난 줄 아는 거였다. 이불깃 위로 대머리 진 이마만 보이는 아버지가 밭은기침을 쏟았다. 또다시 따스했다가 이내 척척해진 오줌 방울이 허벅지를 타고 흘렀다.

"예에……"

뒤꿈치가 헤진 아버지의 낡은 털신을 끌고 사개가 잘 맞지 않아 삐그덕거리는 부엌문을 열며 한 발짝 덜퍽 내딛자 차가운 눈가루가 신발등 위를 덮쳤다. 간밤에

mother was still asleep. I scared easily. I thought about waking my brother, but he was a deep morning sleeper and wasn't likely to help me, while my pride wouldn't allow me to ask my sister. So there I was, sweating up a storm, with my legs crossed like a twisted pastry and my spine bent so hard I felt it might break. When a few drops of pee leaked out and warmed my thighs, I decided I had to choose whether to wake up Mother and get chewed out, or brave alone to the outhouse that stood at the very end of the nine-family "train house." I chose the latter, to be without consequences.

"Are you going somewhere...?"

"N-no..."

"Then why are you in your *uwagi*[1)]... There's cooled *sungnyung* in the rice pot next to the fireplace in the kitchen."

After leaning her head back from the door to say this, Mom pulled her blanket back up. I could see her breath in the air. She must have thought that I was thirsty. Father coughed drily a few times, his bald head peeping out from the top of his blanket. A few more drops of pee rolled down my thighs, initially warm then quickly turning cold.

내린 눈이 기찻집의 기다란 마당을 곱게 덮어버린 것이었다. 눈빛 때문에 사위는 생각보다 희부윰했다. 오줌보를 미어뜨릴 듯하던 팽만감도 조금 너누룩해졌다.

나는 낡은 털신 밑에서 뽀드득거리는 소리가 나도록 성큼성큼 무릎을 들어 발걸음을 옮겼다. 그리고 아홉 가구가 함께 쓰는 변소 문을 열고 문턱에 올라 두 번씩이나 푸드덕푸드덕 몸서리를 치며 오줌을 갈겼다. 이빨을 위아래로 서너 번 맞부딪치며 뽑아내는 오줌 줄기가 원뿔형으로 딱딱하게 굳은 언 똥에 둔탁하게 달라붙는 소리가 들렸다. 곧이어 따스한 오줌 세례를 받은 언 똥이 물컹물컹하게 녹아내리는 소리를 눈을 지그시 감고 듣다가 김이 되어 무럭무럭 콧속을 파고드는 지린내에 코를 쫑긋거리며 돌아나온 것까지는 좋았다.

바지춤을 추스리며 김장독을 가지런히 묻어둔 곁을 어정어정 걸어 나오다가 발끝으로 눈 덮인 가마니때기 밑에서 뭔가 묵직한 것을 밟았다. 가마니때기 속에 발을 담근 채 눈을 폭 뒤집어쓰고 벽에 기대 있던 그 기다란 물체는 고개를 발딱 젖히는가 싶더니 옆으로 풀썩 쓰러졌다. 눈이 털려나간 그 물체는 공사판에서 쓰는 빠루라는 연장이었다. 어른 엄지보다도 굵은 그 기다란

"OK..."

Sliding in my father's old fur-trimmed slippers with worn-out heels, I pushed open the kitchen door that squeaked from its ill-fitting dovetail joints, and took a step forward, only to have cold snow powder splatter my shoes. Snow had fallen overnight to cover the length of the train house's front yard. Thanks to the snow, the surroundings were not as dark as I'd expected. The swelling that had threatened to tear my bladder open also eased up a bit.

I walked on swiftly, lifting my knees enough to make soft, wet noises with the old shoes. Then I opened the door of the communal outhouse, stood on the threshold, and pissed away, shuddering. Along with the sound of my chattering teeth, I heard the stream of my urine pound and coat the cone-shaped pile of frozen feces. Soon I savored, with my eyes closed, the sound of the frozen feces slowly melting. Then I turned to leave, my nose now twitching from the stink of urine that had entered my nostrils as steam. Everything was fine up until this point.

As I straightened my pants and strolled by the row of buried winter kimchi pots, I stepped on

쇠뭉치는 지렛대로 쓰였는데 끝이 물음표처럼 생겼고 또 갈래가 져서 대못 같은 것을 빼는 데 아주 쓸모가 있었다. 그런데 그 빠루가 넘어지면서 하필이면 땅속에 묻지 않고 그냥 바깥에 놔둔 조그마한 짠지 단지를 스치자 뚜껑은 두 동강이 나 떨어졌고 몸통에는 왕금이 좌악 그어졌다. 금은 갔지만 그 짠지 단지가 당장 두 쪽으로 갈라질 것 같진 않았다. 하지만 그 갈라진 틈새에서는 시금털털한 김치 냄새를 풍기는 국물이 쨀끔쨀끔 새어나오고 있었다.

사태는 명백하고도 돌이킬 수가 없었다. 일어나서는 안 되는 일을 저지른 것이었다. 나는 삭풍이 부는 황량한 벌판으로 변한 마당가에 서서 힘이 쭈욱 빠져나간 두 어깨를 거느리며 고개를 젖혀 하늘을 바라보았다. 오오, 하느님 지금 무슨 일이 벌어진 것입니까! 그러나 무거운 눈을 밤새 다 털어버린 새벽하늘은 너무 높이 올라가 있어 내 혼잣소리가 도저히 닿을 수 없었다. 고개를 숙였다. 나는 시치미를 떼고 누워 있는 그 시커먼 빠루가 마치 마녀의 주문을 받아 밤새 뿌린 눈송이를 덮고 위장한 채 기다리다가 내 발길을 일부러 잡아채지나 않았는가 하는 엉뚱한 의심이 들 정도였다.

something hefty under a snow-covered straw sack. The long object had been leaning against the wall, swathed in snow with its feet tucked inside the straw sack, when it suddenly stood up, then fell over sideways. With the snow gone, I saw that it was a tool used in construction, a *pparu*[2)]. This long metal pipe, thicker than an adult's thumb, was used as a lever. It had a curved, forked end, very handy for tearing out things like large nails. On its way down, the *pparu* had grazed, of all things, a little pickle jar that was sitting outside instead of being buried. The lid came away in two pieces, and there was a crack running through its body. Although there was a sharp line running down it from top to bottom, the jar didn't split in two right away. But the sour, salty water from the pickled radishes was already seeping out.

The situation was clear and irreversible. I had done that which must never be done. Standing at the edge of the yard, which had by then become a bitterly windy and desolate moor, I lifted my face to the sky, letting my arms dangle from my lifeless shoulders. Oh, God, what had just happened? The dawn sky, weightless after shedding all that heavy snow overnight, was too high for my words to

나는 어린애답지 않게 몹시 피로하다는 생각이 들었던 듯하다. 그것은 내가 그 순간 헐떡이고 있었던 이유를 적절하게 해명해줄 수 있었다. 피로하다는 것, 이루 말할 수 없는 피로감…… 하긴 어찌 피로하지도 않고 감쪽같이 기절할 수 있겠는가. 바로 그때 내가 피로해야 하는 목적은 두말할 나위 없이 기절하는 것이었다. 기절이라도 하고 나면 이 세상에 뭔가가 달라져 있겠지, 혹은 최소한 모면의 여지는 남겠지 하는 맹렬한 위안이 달라붙었다. 동시에 그 피로감은 어쨌든 세상에 대한 것이라는 게 명백해졌다. 변소에서 오줌보를 비우고 돌아서기까지 나는 너무나 생생했고, 빠루를 밟고 나서 갑자기 피로감을 느끼기까지 불과 십여 초가 흐르는 동안 나는 아무 일도 하지 않았다. 따라서 그 피로감이란 육체적 고단함에서 비롯된 게 아니라 정신적 흔들림에서 우러난 것이 분명했다. 그런 의미에서 그 피로감은 어른에게나 해당하는 피로였다.

한편으로는 그 피로감은 몹시 물리치기 어려운 불길함을 품고 있었다. 몇 해 전 길게 뺀 혓바닥 위에 거꾸로 올려놓은 박탄-D 병의 밑바닥을 손으로 탁탁 두들겨가며 쥐어짠 두어 방울의 알싸한 액체로는 도저히 풀 수

reach. I lowered my head. I had a peculiar suspicion that the *pparu*, now lying there looking innocent, might have been lying in wait all night, camouflaged in snow, as if under a witch's spell, to trip me.

I remember thinking then that I was fatigued, a feeling unbecoming of a child. That would explain why I was panting that moment. That indescribable sense of fatigue... I mean, how could you completely pass out without being fatigued? The point of my fatigue was, without a doubt, passing out. And when I came to, something new would happen in this world, or, at least, there would still be some possibility that I could avoid the unavoidable. This consolation clung to me. At the same time, I was now positive that the fatigue I was feeling was about the world as a whole. After I emptied my bladder in the outhouse I felt absolutely vibrant; then I stepped on the *pparu*, and I did not do any work in the ten seconds or so before fatigue suddenly came over me. So that feeling of fatigue did not spring from physical exhaustion but from mental instability. In that sense, the fatigue I was feeling was only applicable to adults.

At the same time, there was something ominous

없을 것이라는 확신마저 어렸다. 그리고 무엇보다도 앞으로도 오랫동안 그 피로감을 떨쳐낼 수 없을 것이라는 지루한 예감이 그날 어슴푸레한 새벽에 덮친 절망감의 핵심이었다. 문간통에서 두 번째 집구석에 사는 술주정뱅이 고물장수 순심이 아부지의 노상 흐느적거리는 두 팔과 술 때문에 항상 짓물러져 있는 눈자위가 눈앞에 어른거렸다. 아저씨도 나처럼 피로해서 그랬을까? 돌산 밑에서 개를 끄실리다가 덴 손가락에 약국에서 사온 가제를 칭칭 감고 소독을 한답시며 두 홉들이 소주를 다 따른 스뎅 주발 안에 질벅질벅 담그다가 홧김에 그 소주 주발을 잡아채 박탄-D처럼 벌컥벌컥 들이켜던 순심이 아부지도 되게 피로해서 그랬을까.

그런데 그토록 피로한 사람이 왜 뒤늦게 사팔뜨기 여자는 단칸방으로 불러들여 국민학교도 다니지 못하고 실밥 따는 공장에 다니던 순심이를 말이 기숙사지 공장의 골방으로 내보내고 배추 장수가 꿈이던 상준이를 이미 개가한 전처 집으로 억지로 떠맡겨 보내 세상살이의 피로감을 되레 가중시켰는지 모를 일이었다. 그렇게 새로 낸 살림이 채 일 년도 가지 못해 계집이 달아나 깨지고, 오도 가도 못하게 된 순심이 아부지가 하필 겨울이

about my fatigue that I couldn't shake. Even a few bittersweet drops of Baktan-D[3)] that I had once managed to get on my tongue a few years before by tapping the bottom of the bottle wouldn't be able to make it go away. More than anything, at the core of the despair that came over me on that gray-white dawn was a tedious premonition that I wouldn't be able to get rid of the fatigue for a long time to come. I could picture Sun-sim's drunk of a father, a junkman who lived in the second room, arms flailing and eyes bleary from constant boozing. Was he fatigued like me? When he wrapped his finger with gauze after he'd burned it broiling dog meat at the foot of a stone hill, then "disinfected" it by dunking it in a stainless steel bowl filled with a gallon of *soju*, but ended up picking up the bowl and drinking the whole thing like it was Baktan-D, was it because of terrible fatigue?

But if he was so fatigued, then why he shacked up later with the cross-eyed woman in the room he shared with the kids, eventually driving Sun-sim to the closet of a room in the so-called dormitory at the sweatshop when she had already been plucking threads there instead of going to elementary school, and pushing Sang-jun, who dreamed

닥쳐 일도 안 나가고 전세 보증금을 야금야금 까먹다 또 종무소식이 된 걸 두고, 엄마는 새로 온 여자가 수돗가에서 스뎅 요강을 부시다 내리쳐 찌그러뜨렸기 때문이라며 끌탕을 했다.

엄마가 남의 딱한 사정에 어거지 비슷하게 푸념을 하며 동정의 여지를 누르는 이유는 사실 딴 데 있었다. 순심이 아부지한테 작정을 하고 거금 칠백 원을 들여 산 중고 석유 곤로가 보름도 채 가지 않아 결딴이 났다. 제일 밑에 있는 연료통 바닥이 샜던 것이다. 순심이 아부지는 자기가 넘길 때는 아무런 이상이 없었다고 모르쇠를 딱 잡아뗐지만 엄마는 그렇게 생각하지 않았다. 습기 때문에 너덜너덜 부식한 밑바닥에 난 구멍을 임시방편으로 뻬빠질로 때운 흔적이 있다는 거였다. 그 일 때문에 순심이 아부지에 대한 엄마의 감정이 되돌이킬 수 없을 만큼 상해 있었다. 엄마는 새로 끼워 넣은 하얀 심지를 꺼내 말렸고 됫병에 종이 깔때기를 꽂고 석유 곤로에 남은 기름을 부어넣고 병 입에 신문지를 박박이 쑤셔 넣었다. 그리고 고철값 이백 원을 쳐서 줄 테니 자신한테 넘기라는 순심이 아부지의 말을 귓등으로 듣고 내게 누런 울릉도 호박엿으로 바꿔 먹도록 뜻밖의 승낙

of becoming a cabbage seller, on his ex-wife who was already remarried—which must have only exacerbated that feeling of worldly fatigue—I would never know. When that new life ended because the woman ran away within a year, and Sun-sim's father, out of work in the winter and stuck between a rock and a hard place, started to dip into his security deposit stash before disappearing altogether, Mom rubbed it in, saying how it was all because that new woman had bashed in a stainless steel pot while rinsing it at the faucet in the yard.

There was another reason why Mom withheld her compassion for Sun-sim's father and only offered a barely discernable grumble at another's misfortune. The used kerosene stove we had bought from Sun-sim's father for a monumental sum of 700 *won* broke down within a couple of weeks. The fuel tank on the bottom had a leak. Sun-sim's father claimed there had been absolutely nothing wrong with it at the time of the transaction, but Mom disagreed with him. She contended that there was a trace of a sanded patch-up job over a frayed hole at the bottom of the stove that had eroded from moisture. Because of that incident, Mom's feelings were irreversibly hurt against Sun-

을 했었다.

아버지가 중풍으로 쓰러진 다음날 아침 제일 처음 들렀다가 한의원으로 가라는, 사실상의 진료 거부를 당한 신풍의원 맞은편의 동사무소 옆 골목길을 타고 꾸역꾸역 올라가다보니 길음초등학교 담벼락을 끼고서 마을버스 종점인 콘크리트 물탱크 밑 차부까지 올라갔다. 구 경계선인 한길을 따라 걸어 내려가려니까 왼쪽으로는 임마누엘교회 하나와 구멍가게 한 채를 빼놓고는 이미 철거가 다 끝난 폐허의 등성이뿐이었다. 미처 챙겨가지 못한 망가진 가재도구들이 제멋대로 누워 있는 벽돌 무더기 사이로 사람들이 자근자근 밟고 다녔을 골목길들이 호젓한 산길처럼 구불구불 뻗어나 서로 얽히고설켜 있었다. 무너져 방구들이 내려앉은 집들은 터무니없이 작아 보였다. 사방 서너 발짝쯤이나 될까 한 장방형 방 안에서 살을 맞부빈 식구들이 최소한 넷 아니면 우리처럼 여섯쯤일 수도 있었을 것이다. 이제 막 재개발이 결정된 셋집이 있는 오른편 기슭은 겉으론 아직 옛 모습 그대로인 듯했지만, 이상하게도 인적이 끊긴 듯 적조한 분위기를 풍겼다. 어쩌면 벌써 방을 빼 나간 집주인도 있을지 모를 일이었다.

sim's father. Mom took out the newly-inserted white wick to dry, used a paper funnel to pour the remaining kerosene from the stove into a two-quart bottle, and then plugged it tight with newspaper. Deaf to Sun-sim's father's offer of 200 *won* for the metal, Mom unexpectedly allowed me to exchange it for Ulleungdo pumpkin toffee.

Trudging up the street off of the town hall, across from the Shinpung medical office, where they had virtually refused to treat my father the morning after he'd had a stoke, suggesting he see an acupuncturist instead, I passed by Gireum Elementary School and went all the way to the bus depot by the concrete water tank, the final stop of the town shuttle bus. I walked down the hill along the broad street that used to mark the old town limits and saw that most of the neighborhood on the left was already in post-wreckage ruins. Only Immanuel Church and a small convenience store remained. Streets that hundreds of residents must have graced with their footsteps were now like quiet mountain paths, entwined and weaving through piles of bricks and scattered household items. The houses, their hypocausts collapsed, looked unthinkably tiny. Within a rectangular room

"어머닌 건강하시냐, 어때?"

한길가에서 구멍가게를 겸하고 있는 임씨 아저씨 집 앞을 지나는데 가게 반대쪽 터에서 귀에 익은 목소리가 들려왔다. 나는 반코트 호주머니에서 손을 빼 공손히 고개를 숙였다.

"예에…… 안녕하세요?"

머리가 허옇게 센 임씨 아저씨와 대충 얼굴은 알 만한 술꾼들 네댓이 가게 앞 철거된 집터에서 자그마하게 모닥불을 피우고 모여 앉아 있었다. 그 위에 걸친 프라이팬에서 삼겹살을 굽는 연기가 피어올랐다. 대충 짐작컨대 예전의 88이발관 자리였다. 다들 불콰한 얼굴이었다. 철거하고 남은 터라 그런지 부서진 장롱, 의자 다리, 문설주 등등 모닥불에 넣을 나무 쪼가리 지천이어서 그저 안주거리만 있으면 술추렴을 해서 한낮 거나하게 흔전만전 보내기 맞춤인 나날이었다.

"어딜 바쁘게 가?"

"아유, 아닙니다. 바쁘긴요. 그냥 한번 들렀습니다."

"그렇지. 이젠 들를 때가 되긴 됐지."

임씨는 고개를 무던하게 끄덕이다 프라이팬에서 올라온 연기에 눈가를 구기며 고기를 한 점 집어 깨소금

only several steps wide, a family of four, or, in my case, a family of six could have lived, falling over one another. On the right side of the hill, in the neighborhood with the rental property that had just been approved for redevelopment, things seemed the same as before; yet there was this odd sense of absence. Perhaps there were some landlords who had already had their properties vacated.

"How's your mother doing? Good?"

A familiar voice stopped me from the lot across the street. I was passing in front of Mr. Yim's house, which doubled as a convenience store by the broad street. I took my hands out of my coat pockets and bowed politely.

"Uh, yes... how are you?"

A white-haired Mr. Yim was sitting around a small bonfire in the lot of a demolished house in front of the store, with four or five drinking buddies who were somewhat familiar to me. Smoke rose up from the pork belly frying in a pan over open flames. I guessed the spot as the lot where 88 Barbershop had been. The men's faces were all florid. With an abundance of available firewood—broken armoires, chair legs, and doorposts leftover after demolition—booze and a little something to

종지 안에 휘저었다. 옆에서는 고깃점을 양념빛이 좋은 김치에 싸서 길게 뺀 혓바닥 위에 실었다.

"형은 아랫집에 있죠?"

"지금 개 데리고 돌산에 똥 뉘러 갔을 게야. 보다시피 아래루다 말짱 바숴놨으니깐 아무데서나 누이라고 해도 운동 삼아 간다니 뭐. 곧 올 게야. 그건 그렇고 정 바쁘지 않다고 했으니 이리 와서 술이나 한잔해라 너!"

"아, 예……"

방울 달린 벙거지를 쓴 사내가 엉덩이를 들었다 놓으며 모닥불 앞으로 끼어들 틈새를 열어주는 시늉을 했다. 나는 곱은 손을 숯잉걸 앞으로 들이밀었다.

"너 우리 창이 만난 지 꽤나 된 모양이구나. 그치?"

"아, 예 그동안 제가……"

"쩝, 이따 만나서 얘기 좀 나누면 되겠지."

흔적 없이 무너져내린 집터에서 벽돌을 엉덩이 밑에 깔거나 듬성듬성 속이 터진 비닐 소파에 뭉개고 앉아 벽돌 위에 프라이팬을 걸고 낮술을 마시는 광경이 전혀 어색하지 않고 오히려 잘 어울릴 지경이었다. 폐허와 술! 그 광경을 보지 못한 사람은 아마 어떤 허무적인 정조를 떠올릴지 모르나 그것은 야릇하게도 정반대의 느

go with it was all one needed in those days for an afternoon of indulgent drinking.

"Where're you headed in such a hurry?"

"Oh, no, I'm in no hurry. I just wanted to drop by."

"Of course. It was about time."

Nodding his head obligingly, Mr. Yim picked up a piece of meat, his eyes squinting from the rising smoke, and rolled it around in sesame powder. The man beside him was putting meat wrapped in well-seasoned kimchi onto his outstretched tongue.

"Chang is in the house down the road, right?"

"He should be up in the stone hill walking the dog. I tell him the dog can take a dump anywhere, what with all the wreckage down there, but he says he wants to exercise, so what can I say? He should be back soon. Enough about that. You're not in a hurry, you say? Come over here and have a glass, will you?"

"Oh, OK..."

The man in the bobble cap feigned moving over by lifting his rear slightly so that I could get near the fire. I shoved my stiff hands in front of the burning charcoal.

낌을 띠었다. 묘한 활력이라고나 할까. 기름기가 자글자글 흐르는 육질 안주 때문인지 술 한잔에 목을 빼고 걸근거리던 꾀죄죄한 술꾼들의 얼굴이 이미 아니었다. 그들의 얼굴에 궁기라고는 찾아볼 수 없었다. 앞으로 한 해, 아니 길게 잡으면 두 해쯤은 재개발 경기의 훈풍이 그들의 버즘꽃 핀 얼굴에 개기름이나마 번드르하게 발라줄 수 있을지 모른다.

"없어, 남은 거 없어……"

내가 귀 기울이지 않는 사이에 누군가 입을 쩝쩝거리며 푸념했다. 딱지 거래 얘긴가 싶어 고개를 돌렸더니 빈 소주병을 잡고 흔들었다.

"이번엔 당신이 한 두어 병 사. 이 참에 나 술장사 좀 하게."

임씨 아저씨가 농을 던지자 기다렸다는 듯 막 이발을 했는지 자를 대고 그은 듯 곧바르게 가르마를 탄 머리에 기름기가 번들거리는 사내가 호주머니에서 구깃구깃한 천 원짜리를 두어 장 꺼내 던졌다. 임씨 아저씨가 아무렇지도 않은 표정으로 챙겨 넣고는 가게로 가 소주병을 들고 돌아오며 가르마 탄 사내에게 물었다.

"웬 찍다 남은 벼루를 그렇게 많이 두고 갔어? 어제

"It must have been quite a while since you last saw Chang."

"Well, yes, I've been..."

"Shoot, you guys can have a chat when you see him."

Sitting on a brick or a vinyl-covered couch, its filling coming out here and there, in the lot of a completely demolished house, and having drinks in the middle of the day, with a frying pan hanging over bricks, actually made for a quite harmonious view, not out of place at all. Drinks amidst the ruins! That combination might have evoked some sort of nihilistic sentiment to those without first-hand experience. But, curiously enough, the atmosphere was decidedly the opposite. One might have called it an eerie liveliness. Perhaps it was from the meat dripping with fat, but the men gathered there no longer looked like their former grimy selves, abjectly vying for a sip of booze. Not a trace of want appeared on their faces. In a year, two at the most, a favorable fallout from the redevelopment-aided market might grease up their psoriasis-adorned faces.

"None, nothing left..."

While I wasn't paying attention, someone had

그저께까지만 해도 애들이 벽돌 틈새를 안 뒤지나 난리들이었어."

"그럼 뭘 해? 그깟 세멘또 덩어리 짐만 되지."

그제야 나는 그 가르마 탄 사내가 88이발소 옆 담벼락 밑에 지붕이 폭 빠진 자그마한 가내 벼루 공장 사내임을 알아보았다. 불과 며칠 전에 집을 허물고 딴 곳으로 옮긴 눈치였다.

"편지가 아직 여기 허물어진 집주소로 오는감?"

"에이구 딴 건 필요 없구…… 오늘니알 중으로 거시키 받을 게 있어서 이렇게 자리를 지키는 거여, 커어."

그만 일어나야겠다고 생각하는데 마침 개를 끌고 내려오는 창이 형이 멀찌감치 보였다.

"민홍이 왔구나!"

나는 엉거주춤한 자세로 한 손을 높이 들었다.

"형 얼굴이 많이 좋아 보이는데요. 근데 이놈 그새 많이도 늙었네요."

"이젠 눈독 들이는 사람도 없어."

"무슨 눈독이요? 종자 더 못 쳐요?"

그 개는 온 동네 암캐한테 흘레를 붙여주는 종자 개였다.

grumbled, smacking his lips. I turned my head wondering if he was referring to deeds for sale and saw that he was waving an empty *soju* bottle.

"You take this round so I can play bar owner."

Prompted by Mr. Yim's quip, a man, his pomaded hair so perfectly-parted it looked he had just stepped out of a barber shop, took out a couple of crumpled thousand-*won* bills from his pocket and tossed them on the table. Straightfaced, Mr. Yim grabbed them and disappeared inside the store, and then on his way out, holding *soju* bottles, called out to the guy with the perfectly parted hair:

"Gee, look how many unfinished ink stones you left here! Up until a couple days ago, kids were going crazy for them, even searching between the bricks and all."

"Why should I take 'em? Those cemento[4)] slabs would only be dead weight."

Only then did I realize the guy with the parted hair used to make ink stones out of his house with the caved-in roof next to 88 Barbershop. He must have moved out just days before after having his house razed.

"Still getting mail sent to this leveled house?"

"No that doesn't matter... I'm just waiting here

"그것도 그렇고 요즘 여기 개가 흔해서 사람들이 심심찮게 개를 꼬실려 먹거든."

"아무래도 경기가 좋아지니까 그간 입에 못 대던 개고기가 날개 돋친 듯하나요?"

"그게 아니고 저 동네 집 다 부수고 나서 임자 잃은 개도 많고 하니깐 먼저 보고 때려잡는 놈이 장땡이지. 저건 뭔 거 같니?"

"그럼 저게……"

"헤에, 아침녘에 발발이 하나 잘못 걸려들어서 바로 매달았지. 냄새 맡아보면 알 텐데."

"멍멍이 고기도 돼지고기처럼 구워 먹어요?"

"그게 또 별미래. 이놈 빨리 집 안으로 들여서 묶어놔야겠어. 같은 종족 살점 굽는 냄새 맡으니깐 흰자위가 돌아가고 뒷다리에 바들바들 힘주고 성질부리려 드는데. 참 어머니께서 집 내놓으셨다 도로 거둬들이셨데?"

"아, 그거요? 그런 모양이던데 전 잘 몰라요. 어머니 명의로 돼 있잖아요."

"그거 잘하셨어. 파시더라도 내년까지 최고로 오를 때까지 기달려야지. 너랑 같이 사시니깐 당장 뭐 큰돈 필요한 건 없으시지?"

cause I need to get the whatchamacallit from them any day now, keh keh keh."

Just as I was about to get up, I saw Chang come down the hill with his dog.

"Hey there, Min-hong!"

I raised my arm from my half-squat position.

"You're looking good, Chang. And this guy here, he's getting up there in years now, huh?"

"Nobody's even giving him a second look nowadays."

"Second look? You're not breeding him anymore?"

The dog was a stud dog used for mating with all the bitches in town.

"No, but with lots of dogs around here these days, people have taken to broiling them for meat."

"Hmm, now that the market is booming, is dog meat going like hotcakes? Even though no one could stomach it before?"

"That's not it. When all those houses were torn down, a lot of dogs were left behind. So whoever got to them first got to eat them. What do you think you're cooking there?"

"So this is..."

"Yup, we had a poor lost pooch wander in here

"아, 예…… 그것도 그렇구요, 전 그 셋집 아저씨가 보일러 고쳤다고 어쩌구 구시렁대기도 하고 또 아버지 영정 사진도 아직 거기 골방 구석에 처박혀 있고 그래서요…… 겸사겸사."

"아암, 아무튼 좋아."

그동안 형은 몸이 골골한데다 직장 없이 가끔씩 아버지 가게에서 석유나 연탄 배달을 해주며 개나 벗 삼고 지내온지라 낼 모레 마흔 줄을 앞두고도 장가를 들지 못했다. 나는 그런 창이 형한테서 예전과 달리 풍기는 활력의 정체를 형이 따로 방을 내서 사는 데를 가보고서야 알았다. 올봄에 내가 들렀던 사랑방교회 위의 허름한 방이 아니었다. 형은 한길을 좀더 타고 내려가다 정육점과 슈퍼 비디오점 미장원이 모인 거리에 있는 연립주택의 반지하방으로 나를 이끌었다.

"형, 방 옮겼어요?"

"응, 너 점심이라도 먹고 가야지."

창이 형은 성실정육점에 들러 돼지고기 한 근을 썰어 달라고 했다.

"형은 네 발 달린 고기 잘 안 먹는 등 푸른 생선파잖아요?"

this morning so we hung it right away. What, you can't tell from the smell?"

"So you roast doggies like you do with pigs?"

"Supposedly a delicacy. I'd better bring this guy in and tie him up. See how his eyes are rolling back and he's pushing off on his hind legs, ready to throw a fit? He must be smelling his brethren getting grilled. Oh, yeah, I saw that your mother's pulled her property off the market."

"Oh, that. Yeah, I guess so; I'm not too familiar with that. It's in her name, you know."

"She's being smart. But she should wait till next year anyway before thinking about selling it, when the prices peak. It's not like she needs a big sum of cash right now since she's living with you, right?"

"Oh, right... that, too. Plus, the tenant there has been going on and on about fixing the boiler, and I might as well grab my father's funeral portrait that was stashed in there somewhere... so, I'm here for this and that."

"Sure, that's all good."

Chang was sickly by nature and jobless other than making occasional fuel deliveries for his father's store. He had still been single a couple of years away from turning forty, with a dog as his only

"식성이란 변하게 마련 아냐. 부쩍 근력이 달려서 요즘 육질을 입에 많이 대는 편이지. 사람 입이 간사해서 자꾸 먹어보니깐 또 먹을 만해져."

형의 뒤를 따라 현관문을 들어서는 순간 으레 코를 찌르던 쉬어터진 홀아비 냄새가 풍기지 않았다. 그것보다 반짝반짝 빛나는 휴지통을 필두로 내 눈앞에 펼쳐진 규모 있는 살림집의 모습이 나를 잠시 당혹스럽게 만들었다. 부쩍 근력이 달린다는 형의 말이 무슨 뜻인지 알 듯했다.

"이 사람이 밥 먹고 또 자는 모양이지?"

"예에…… 아니 형 그럼 혹시……."

"올 여름에 그냥 도둑장가 들어버렸지 뭐 헤헤."

"왜 연락을……."

"식은 안 올리고……."

나는 놀라움보다 반가움이 앞서서 입을 쩍 벌리며 뒤에서 형의 두 어깨를 끌어안았다. 그때 방문이 열리면서 아직 잠기가 가시지 않은 눈매를 한 여자가 부스스한 퍼머 뒷머리를 긁으며 원피스 잠옷 차림으로 나왔다. 나도 제법 안면이 있는 여자였다.

"형수님 안녕하세요? 인사 올립니다."

companion. So Chang's air of vitality, something I hadn't felt before, didn't make sense to me until we arrived at his new place. It wasn't the beat-up room above Sarangbang Church I'd visited in the spring. After walking down the hill farther along the street, he led me into the half-basement of a multi-family house. There was a butcher shop, a grocery store, a video store, and a hair salon on the same block.

"Chang, you got a new pad?"

"Yeah. Why don't you stay for lunch?"

We dropped by Seongsil Butcher Shop, where Chang got a pound and a half of pork sliced.

"I thought you only ate blue-backed fish and never hoofed animals?"

"Palates change, you know. I'm eating a lot of meat these days to boost my low stamina. I guess human appetite is a fickle thing. I'm kind of enjoying it now."

There was no trace of the familiar rancid man smell when I followed him inside his home. Not only that, I was momentarily confounded by the sight of a respectable-sized space, starting with a gleaming wastebasket in the corner. I was beginning to grasp what he'd meant by his "low stamina."

"어머나, 챙피, 이를 어째! 오늘 아침따라 얼굴에 물칠도 못 하고…… 아, 누군가 했더니 저기 가겟집 할머니 막내아들 아네요?"

"왜 아닙니까 하하. 늦었지만 두 분께 진심으로 축하드립니다."

나는 한껏 너스레를 떨었다.

"이거 목살 썰어온 거예요. 그냥 소금구이로 해주실래요?"

깍듯한 존댓말을 붙이는 형의 얼굴에 어린애처럼 마냥 천진난만한 미소가 잠시 어렸다. 여자의 퍼머머리를 단발머리로 바꾸어 머릿속에 그려보자 비로소 이름이 떠올랐다. 국희일 것이다. 미아리 셋집 옆의 구두집 문간방에 살던 효상이 엄마의 동생. 어머니가 국희라고 대뜸 이름으로 불렀던 그 단발머리 아가씨는 처음엔 재봉사였다.

우리 집 뒤의 마당 넓은 집이 한때 바느질집을 할 때 효상이 엄마가 자신의 동생을 소개해서 효상이네 다락방에서 자면서 그 집 대문으로 한동안 들락거렸다. 땅딸막한 몸매에 얼굴도 오막오막하게 생겼지만 목덜미에 잔털이 비치도록 귀밑까지 바짝 깎아올린 단발머리

"She must have gone back to sleep after the meal," said Chang abruptly.

"What... wait, Chang, then are you..."

"I got hitched over the summer. In secret," he laughed.

"Why didn't you tell me?"

"We didn't have a wedding."

More glad for him than surprised, I hugged Chang around his shoulders from behind, my mouth hanging open. Just then the bedroom door opened and out came a woman in a cotton night-gown with her eyes still half-closed, scratching the back of her frizzy-permed hair. She was someone I recognized as well.

"Hello, Sis. How are you?" I said.

"Oh my, I'm so embarrassed! Goodness, I haven't even washed my face this morning... Oh, I remember you now. Aren't you the younger son of the old lady with that store?"

"Who else would I be?" I laughed. "Please accept my belated heartfelt congratulations."

I carried on like an idiot.

"I got some sliced neck meat from the butcher," Chang told his wife. "Do you think you could grill it with just salt, please?"

가 인상적이었다. 당시 나는 대학생이었다. 이따금 엄마의 구멍가게에 와서 새참으로 단팥빵이나 알밤케익을 나한테 돈을 주고 사서 선 자리에서 눈만 깜짝깜짝거리며 먹곤 돌아갔다. 실밥이 잔뜩 묻은 헐렁한 면바지의 무릎은 풍덩 빠져 있었고 굵은 허리까지 내려온 옷의 밑 단추가 가끔 하나씩 풀려 있었지만, 빵을 잔뜩 베문 뽀얀 양 볼따구니 밑으로는 파란 거머리 같은 실핏줄이 해맑게 비쳤다. 나는 그 볼따구니를 흘깃흘깃 훔쳐보느라 요구르트 하나 값을 계산에서 빠뜨릴 적이 많았다.

내가 미국 레이건 대통령 방한 반대 가두시위 중 종로 3가에서 연행돼 구류를 살고 나온 동안 그 처제는 어디론가 가고 없었다. 엄마는 내가 들을세라 말세라 어쩐지 그 입술 시퍼런 게 사내깨나 후리게 생겼더라 어쩌구 하면서 구시렁거렸다. 며칠간 동네를 세게 휘젓고 간 사건이 벌어진 모양이었다. 형부와 처제가 붙어먹었다는 내용이었다. 그 가공할 풍문 덕택에 내가 데모를 하다 나흘간 유치장에 있다 나온 사건은 동네에서 흔적도 없이 휩쓸려갔다. 나중엔 결국 정식으로 이혼을 했지만 그때 죽네 못 사네 하던 효상이네 부부도 겨우

Chang was speaking in polite honorifics. He briefly beamed, with a sweet smile of a child. I looked at Chang's wife again. When I pictured her in my head, substituting a straight bob for her perm, I remembered her name. It had to be Guk-hee. She was the younger sister of Hyo-sang's mom. Hyo-sang's mom lived in the room off the entrance to the shoe store next to the Miari house where we were once tenants. The young woman with the short bob, whom my mother had immediately taken to calling by her first name, started out as a seamstress.

When the family in the house with the big yard behind ours had a sewing business for a while, Hyo-sang's mom got her sister a job. So she worked in that house while sleeping in the attic of the house where Hyo-sang's family lived. While she was rather dumpy and had undefined features, I remembered vividly the fuzz of hair at the nape of her neck underneath the short bob that barely covered her ears. I was in university then. She would sometimes come by my mom's tiny store on her break, and buy a red bean or chestnut pastry from me. She would eat it standing right there, just blinking her eyes, before going back. Though her

내 별거를 하더니 이듬해 봄에 다시 합방을 했다. 그 뒤로 효상이 엄마는 자기 동생이 원래 품행이 방정치 못하다고 동네방네 입에 욕을 달고 다녔다.

몇 년 뒤 내가 방위생활을 할 때 단발머리는 돌아왔다. 아니, 긴 머리가 돼 있었다. 그리고 내가 유격훈련을 받느라고 도시락도 싸가지고 다니지 않던 여름철이었다.

"방우 학생, 히힛!"

그녀가 후줄근한 모습으로 부대에서 돌아오던 날 밤 날 불렀다. 알전구 빛이 짱짱하게 내비치는 호남상회 앞 나무 평상 위에 다리를 꼬고 걸터앉은 모습이었다. 석계역 앞 포장마차에서 동기들과 오백 원 빵으로 소주를 한 병쯤 걸친 취기 때문인지 그날따라 심하게 받은 피티 체조 때문인지, 아무튼 오르막에 코를 박고 오르는 호흡이 거칠었다. 신경이 곤두서 있던 나는 땅바닥에 침을 퉤 뱉는 시늉을 하며 스스럼없이 다가서서 감자와 양파가 반쯤 담긴 라면 박스를 밀치고 평상에 엉덩이를 걸쳤다. 동네에서 오며가며 얼굴 마주칠 기회는 많았지만 서로 인사를 할 만한 숫기도 또 그럴 필요도 없었다. 그녀가 내 코앞으로 방금 딴 차가운 코카콜라 한 병을 내밀었다. 갑자기 목젖을 우그러뜨린 갈증이

loose cotton pants were baggy at the knees and covered with loose threads, and though the tops covering her thick waist often had a lower button or two missing, I could see her blue, leech-like capillaries underneath her milky, translucent cheeks, puffy with a mouthful of pastry. Quite often, I would forget to charge for a yogurt or two while stealing glances at those cheeks.

While I was in detention after getting arrested on Jongno-3-ga for marching in protest against President Reagan's visit to Korea, the young woman disappeared. Mom kept harping on about how the girl had always looked like a man-eater with her blue-tinted lips, whether I wanted to hear it or not. A huge scandle involving her had taken the town by storm for a few days. People said she had had an affair with her sister's husband. Thanks to that rumor, the story of my arrest and detention got swept away without a trace. Hyo-sang's parents, who said they couldn't live together anymore by then, separated before getting back together again in the following spring. Eventually, though, they divorced. After that, Hyo-sang's mom went around badmouthing her sister for having never been prim or proper.

나도 모르게 그 병의 잘록한 허리를 덥석 잡게 만들었던 것 같다.

"고생이 많은가 봐요."

한번 반말이면 끝까지 갈 것이지 웬 또 경어람! 그녀가 여러 남정네들을 요정냈다는 소문은 이미 듣고 있었다. 요즘 말로 하자면 꽃뱀이었다. 유부남과 붙어놓고는 돈을 뜯었다는 것이다. 나는 대꾸 없이 병을 입속에 꽂고 난 뒤 사레가 들려 기침을 자지러지게 했다. 사실 콜라를 병째로 마시려고 시도한 건 그때가 처음이었다. 고통스런 기침이었지만 마음은 편했다. 그녀는 내 등을 시원스레 두들겨주지도 못하고 두 손을 마주 쥔 채 어쩔 줄 몰라했다. 나는 뭔지 모르지만 재미난 기분이었다. 그녀한테 질펀한 농지거리라도 하고 싶은 심정이었다. 만약 그때 어깨 위로 간신히 달라붙은 줄에 매달린 얇은 윗옷을 거추장스러운 듯 걸치고 있는 두 봉긋한 젖가슴이 벌름벌름 숨을 쉬고 있지 않았고, 그래서 내 아랫도리가 불끈 천막을 치지만 않았더래도 말이다. 나는 바지 주머니에서 동전 이백 원을 꺼내 평상에 내려놓고 일어섰다. 뒤에서 욕이 튀었다.

"쌍새끼!"

The young woman with the bob reappeared a few years later, by which time I was doing military service in the Korean National Guard. She had long hair by then. It was summertime when I didn't even pack my lunch for my commando training.

"Hey there, nashnul guard student, teehee!"

The woman called me one night as I was coming home, looking sloppy from the camp. She was sitting crossed-legged on the wooden bench in front of Honam Market, lit harshly by a bare light bulb. Perhaps it was the buzz from the bottle of *soju* my campmates and I had just downed by chipping in five hundred *won* each to buy a few bottles at the street cart in front of Seokgye Station, or it might have been the harsher-than-normal physical training exercises earlier that day. For whichever reason, I was breathing heavily as I walked up the hill. Already on edge, I pretended to spit on the ground as I went over without hesitation and put my butt down on the bench, pushing aside a cardboard ramen box half-filled with potatoes and onions. Though we had crossed paths numerous times in the neighborhood, we had neither had the guts nor the need to exchange greetings. She thrust a freshly-opened bottle of ice-cold cola in front of

욕과 동시에 동전 하나가 뒤통수를 알딸딸하게 파고 들었다. 나는 입술을 종그렸다.

"쐐년!"

그러나 뒤돌아보진 않았다. 슬그머니 맥이 풀어졌기 때문이다.

창이 형이 그런 사실을 모를 리가 없었다. 내가 알고 있는 것은 벌써 형이 다 알고 있는 사실일 터이고, 형이 이미 알고 있다면 그건 어떻게 달리 부를 말이 없지 않을까. 운명이라고 할밖에는. 창이 형과 나는 소금구이에 맥주를 퍼마시고 또 놀러 오라는 형수의 말을 뒤로 하고 나왔다. 형은 파출소 건너편에 있는 재개발조합 사무실로 가기 위해 마을버스 돌산 종점으로 올라가는 길이었다.

"형, 늦은 신혼 재미가 어때요? 좋죠?"

순전히 술김이었다. 나는 돼지기름 때문에 더부룩한 배를 쓰다듬으며 물었다.

"헹, 좋냐구? 너도 알다시피 내가 개를 오래 길러봐서 아는데 사실은 사람도 짐승하고 크게 다르지 않을걸. 목숨이 끊어지지 않는 한 야만이면 야만인대로…… 그런데 사람한테는 어쩔 수 없이 미운 정도 있고 고운 정

my nose. Struck by a sudden thrist, I briskly grabbed the bottle at its tapered waist.

"I take it that it's pretty rough for you?"

She had started with a casual tone, but now she was using honorifics! I had heard the stories of the many men she had done in. In today's vocabulary, she was a gold digger. They said she'd seduced and extorted married men. Without answering her, I shoved the bottle in my mouth and had a coughing fit when it went down the wrong tube. That was the fist time I'd ever tried to knock back an entire bottle of cola at once. As painful as the coughs were, my heart was at ease. Seemingly unable to slap me on the back, the girl stood by helplessly with her hands clutched together. Somehow I was having fun. I felt like cracking a risqué joke to her. That is, if the two sweet mounds on her chest hadn't been huffing and puffing under the thin yet cumbersome blouse barely hanging by the straps over her shoulders, and if, as a result, I hadn't pitched a tent in my pants. I took out a couple of coins from my pocket, put them on the bench, and got up. Obscenities shot up from behind.

"Fucking bastard!"

도 있는 거니깐 그거 한 가지 다르다고나 할까…….”

나는 으스스 끝에 몰려온 현훈(眩暈) 때문에 눈앞이 캄캄해졌다. 그 캄캄함 속에서 오래전에 내가 깬 짠지 단지가 두둥실 떠올라주었다. 나는 아직 다 쓰러지지 않은 길가의 전봇대에 시린 이마를 대며 중얼거렸다. 가자……!

그 한마디에 동화 속 같던 온 세상이 한순간에 흰빛 절망감의 구렁텅이로 변하던 장석조네 집 마당에서 어쩔 줄 모르던 소년의 모습이 환하게 떠올랐다.

나는 깨진 단지를 눈으로 찬찬히 확인하는 순간 입술을 파르르 떨었다. 어찌 떨지 않을 수 있었을까. 그 단지의 임자가 욕쟁이 함경도 할머니임에 틀림없음에랴! 이 베락 맞아 뒈질 놈의 아새끼 봤나, 하는 욕설이 귀에 쟁쟁해지자 등 뒤에서 올라온 뜨뜻한 열기가 목덜미와 정수리께를 휩싸며 치솟아 올라 추운 줄도 몰랐다. 눈을 비비고 또 비볐지만 이미 벌어진 현실이 눈앞에서 사라져줄 리는 만무했다.

집 안팎에서 귀청이 떨어져라 퍼부어질 지청구와 매타작을 감수하는 게 상수인 듯싶었다. 아무도 밟지 않은 첫길이라고 일부러 발끝에 힘을 주어 제겨딛고 가느

A coin smacked me in the back of the head. I puckered up my lips.

"Fucking whore!" I yelled, but I did not look back; I had kind of lost my pep.

There was no way Chang didn't know about that night. What I knew, he certainly knew. And if he already knew it, what else could I say about it, other than call it fate?

Chang and I stuffed our faces with salt-grilled meat and beer, then left his home, his wife inviting me to come visit again as I walked out. Chang was going up the stone hill to the town shuttle bus depot in order to get to the office of the redevelopment association across the street from the police substation.

"So Chang, how do you like being an old-bachelor-turned-newlywed? You having fun?"

It was purely the booze talking. I patted my belly, bloated from the fatty pork.

"Fun, you're asking? As you know, I'm sure, I raised dogs for a long time. People are not too different than animals. As long as they're alive, if they are wild, you accept them as wild... though, with people, you develop and collect more and more feelings, through thick and thin. So that's one dif-

라 우리 집 앞에서 변소 앞까지 뚜렷이 파인 눈 위에 내 발자국은 요즘 말로 도주 및 증거 인멸의 가능성을 일찌감치 봉쇄하고 있는 터였다. 이미 아홉 가구의 어느 방 안에서인지 잠에서 깨어난 사람들이 내 행동을 처음부터 끝까지 지켜보기라도 한 양 두런거리는 목소리들이 들려왔다. 나는 울기 전에 최후의 시도를 하기로 맘먹었다. 우랑바리나바롱나르비못다라까따라마까뿌라냐…….

손오공이 부리는 조화를 기대하며 입 속으로 주문을 반복해서 외었다. 그리고는 고개를 홱 돌려 깨진 단지를 내려 보았다. 주문이 헛되지 않았는지 내 입가에 기쁨의 미소가 어렸다. 깨진 단지는 그 모양 그대로였지만 어떤 기발한 생각이 별똥별처럼 머릿속을 스치고 지나갔기 때문이었다. 그렇다 눈사람이다! 나는 가슴이 터질 듯 기뻐 하늘을 향해 두 팔을 쫙 벌렸다. 일단 이 아침만큼은 별일 없이 맞이할 수 있겠지. 나는 장갑도 끼지 않은 손으로 서둘러 주위의 눈을 긁어모으기 시작했다. 마침 찰기가 좋은 눈이어서 손이 한 번 닿을 때마다 흙 알갱이가 알알이 박인 눈덩이들이 붙어 올라왔다. 나는 우선 항아리 주변에 눈사람의 아랫부분을 뭉

ference, I'd say..."

My vision suddenly grew dark and vertigo rushed over me on the heels of the chill. In the darkness appeared the pickle jar I'd broken a long time ago. I steadied my forehead on a cold, roadside utility pole, which had yet to fall down completely.

"Let's go," I said to myself.

With those words I could see again the boy who didn't know what to do in the front yard of Jang Seok-jo's house, which had changed from a fairy-tale world to a pit of despair in an instant.

I remembered how my lips trembled when I confirmed the broken jar with my own hands and eyes. How could they not tremble? Especially when I was positive that it belonged to the granny from Hamgyeong who had one filthy mouth on her. By the time the words "you li'l piece of shit, you shid get struck by lightning and croak!" were ringing in my mind's ears, heat had climbed my back and now rose up, enveloping my neck and head. I forgot all about the cold. No matter how hard I rubbed my eyes, the reality of what had already happened wasn't going to disappear.

My fate was apparently sealed. I would have to endure words of rebuke until my ears fell off or

쳐놓았다. 그리고는 조금 작은 눈덩이를 서둘러 올려놓았다. 그렇게 해서 깨진 단지를 감쪽같이 눈사람 속에 집어넣을 수 있었던 것이다.

"너 벌써부터 나와 노는구나. 부지런하구나."

바로 이웃 방에 사는 현정이 아빠가 담배를 꼬나물고 변소에 가려고 내복 바람으로 나왔다.

"방학 숙제로 낼 일기를 쓰는데요, 눈사람 굴리기라도 해서 적어 넣으려구요. 앞으론 날이 따듯해서 눈사람을 만들려 해도 그러지 못할 거예요. 이것도 금세 녹을걸요."

나는 빨리 집으로 들어가지 않고 내 앞에서 밍기적거려 자꾸 거짓말을 하게 만드는 그가 얄미워졌다. 그 감정을 눙친다고 하는 게 느닷없이 그가 보는 앞에서 눈사람의 귀때기를 조금 떼어내 입에 넣는 행위로 표출되었다. 찝찔한 것 같기도 하고 맹숭한 것 같기도 한 눈 녹은 물을 뱉으려 하자 혀 아래에 흙 알갱이들이 서너 개 걸치적거렸다. 벌써 쉰 줄에 들어선 그가 몇 해 전에 면도사 하는 젊은 마누라를 새로 후려 왔을 때 주변에서는 어떻게 다루려느냐는 시샘 어린 걱정이 많았다. 하지만 베니어판을 사이에 두고 그의 옆방에 살던 꼬마인 나는 한밤중에 자신을 불현듯 깨우곤 하는 숨죽인 앓는

suffer a thrashing in and out of the house. Because I had deliberately stomped hard through the freshly fallen snow, my footsteps appeared cleanly and clearly, leading from our room to the outhouse and eliminating any possibility of fleeing or tampering with the scene. Already, I could hear voices from one of the rooms of the nine families, where someone must have been awake to witness my deed from beginning to end. I made up my mind to make a final attempt before I cried. Abracadabra Narubimottarakkattara Makkappuranya...

I kept repeating the incantation, expecting a miracle like that of Sun Wu-kong. Then I turned my head with a snap in the direction of the broken jar. The magic words hadn't been for naught. A smile came over my face. While the jar was still broken, a spectacular idea flashed through me like a shooting star. A snowman! My heart pounded with jubilation as I threw up my arms toward the sky. I could at least begin the day without any trouble. With my bare hands, I hurriedly set about gathering snow around me. Luckily it was wet snow, and I easily scooped up big lumps of snow with sand and pebbles in them. I put snow around the jar as the bottom of the snowman. Then I quickly placed a

소리의 정체를 알고 있었다. 변소가 떠나갈 듯이 소피를 보고 나온 그는 내가 세운 눈사람을 힐끗 보더니 두터운 입술 새에서 담배를 꺼내 눈사람의 입가에 꽂으며 호탕하게 웃었다. 나도 따라 웃었다. 그러자 기다렸다는 듯이 부엌문들이 차례로 열리기 시작했다.

그 현장을 더 이상 지킬 수 없었던 나는 그날 하루 동안의 가출을 감행하지 않을 수 없었다. 왜냐하면 눈사람 속에 감춰진 비밀이란 영원할 수가 없어서 반나절만 지나면 오후의 찬란한 햇빛 아래 만천하에 드러나게 마련이기 때문이었다. 비밀이란 햇볕을 피해 곰팡이가 피도록 묻혀 있어야 제격인데, 기껏 푸석푸석한 눈덩이에 휩싸인 비밀이란 애초 성립하기 어려운 것이었다.

그 하루 동안 나는 주로 더러운 곳만 골라서 돌아다녔다. 개똥 천지인 돌산길을 돌아 나와, 눈이 녹아 질척거리는 시장거리, 연탄재가 어지럽게 뒹구는 인수교회 뒤쪽의 좁은 골목들을 혼자 떠돌다 딱총용 화약이 숭숭 박인 종이를 두 장 사서 차돌로 터뜨린 다음 콧방울을 벌름벌름하며 한껏 화약내를 맡았다. 가끔 아버지의 아티반을 사러 가는 불란서 약국 뒤의 연탄 가스 냄새가 눈을 찌르는 어두운 단골 만화 가게에서 호주머니를 탈

slightly smaller ball of snow on the top. That was how I was able to move the broken jar inside the snowman.

"Already out playing? An early bird!"

Hyeon-jeong's dad, wearing only long johns, and dangling a cigarette off his lower lip, had stopped on the way to the outhouse from his room next to ours.

"I'm keeping a diary over vacation for homework and I needed something to write about. It's going to get warmer from today, so I don't think I can make any more snowmen even if I want to. This will melt soon, too, I'm sure."

Hyeon-jeong's father said nothing and continued to linger in front of me. I grew annoyed at him for making me tell one lie after another. My attempt to let off some steam inexplicably manifested itself as taking off a bit of the snowman's ear and putting it in my mouth while he watched. When I tried to spit out the partly salty, partly bland melted snow I could feel a few sand particles under my tongue. When Hyeon-jeong's dad managed to lure in a young wife, who worked at a barbershop, those around him envied him and worried how he, already in his 50's, was going to handle her. But I

탈 털어 성인만화를 보며 지금쯤 녹아내렸을 눈사람에 대해 서너 번 생각했다. 마지막 만화책을 처음부터 세 번이나 되풀이 보고 덮고 나올 때 연탄 난로 위에 끓고 있는 떡볶이를 보며 후회했다.

그 길로 처음 볼 땐 한복집인 줄 잘못 알았던 길음천 변의 음산한 텍사스 거리를 겁 없이 걸어다녔다. 그런 용기를 준 것은 허기진 배와 눈사람 속에 묻힌 짠지 단지다. 텍사스 거리의 한쪽 끝에 있는 튀김집 거리를 지날 때는 싸구려 기름 냄새 때문에 뱃속의 내장들이 요동을 치다 못해 밖으로 꾸역꾸역 뛰쳐나올 듯했다. 하지만 설에도 집에 가지 못한 손톱이 긴 매춘부들이 건네주는 오징어 튀김의 유혹에 굴복하진 않았다. 나중에 떨어질 매와 꾸지람을 이겨내기 위해서라도 다른 것은 다 더럽혀져도 자존심만큼은 더럽힐 수 없었다.

그리곤 어느덧 해질녘…… 이미 비밀이 다 까발려졌을 아홉 가구집으로 돌아갔다. 대문간 앞에서 나는 심호흡을 몇 번이고 했다. 엄마한테 연탄집게로 맞으면 안 되는데 싶은 생각뿐이었다. 하지만 내가 대문간 앞을 흐르는 시궁창을 가로지르는 돌다리를 건너갔지만 아무도 나를 보고 아는 체하는 사람이 없었다. 내게 일

slept a veneered wall apart from him, and knew the source of the hushed moans that would wake me in the middle of the night. After he was done pissing a blaring stream in the outhouse, he came back out to look at the snowman. Then he removed the cigarette from between his thick lips, stuck it near the snowman's mouth, and laughed heartily. I laughed, too. Then, as if on cue, kitchen doors began to swing open.

I could not be on the scene any longer. I had no choice but to run away from home for the day. There was no such thing as a permanent secret inside a snowman; after half a day, it would reveal itself to the world under a dazzling afternoon sun. Since secrets were best kept out of the sun, buried deep enough to grow dark and moldy, a secret covered in mushy snow was a difficult scheme from the get-go.

For that whole day, I mainly picked out dirty places to hang out. I walked down the stone hill flowing with dog poop, and roamed alone along the market streets, slushy with melted snow. I wandered through the narrow alleys behind Insu Church, with shattered pieces of used briquettes everywhere. I bought two sheets of firecrackers

제히 안됐다는 시선을 던지며 몰려들었어야 할 사람들이 평소와 다름없이 냄비를 들고 왔다 갔다 했고, 문짝에 기대 입을 가리고 웃었으며, 수돗가에 몰려나와 쌀을 일며 화기애애하게 얘기를 나누고 있었다. 심지어 수돗가에서 시래기를 다듬다 마주친 엄마도 너 점심 굶고 어디 갔다 왔니, 하는 지청구조차 내리지 않았다. 나는 무척 혼돈스러웠다. 사람들이 나를 더 곤혹스럽게 만들기 위해 일부러 짜고 그러는 것도 같았다. 나는 얼른 눈사람을 천연덕스럽게 세워두었던 변소통 쪽을 돌아다보았다. 거기엔 아무것도 없었다. 눈사람은 깨끗이 치워져 있었다. 물론 흉칙한 몰골을 드러내고 있어야 할 짠지 단지도 눈에 띄지 않았다. 도대체 무슨 일이 일어난 것일까?

나는 나를 둘러싼 세계가 너무도 낯설게 느껴졌다. 내가 짐작하고 또 생각하는 세계하고 실제 세계 사이에는 이렇듯 머나먼 거리가 놓여 있었던 것이다. 그 거리감은 사실 이 세계는 나와는 상관없이 돌아간다는 깨달음, 그러므로 나는 결코 주변으로 둘러싸인 중심이 아니라는 아슴프레한 깨달음에 속한 것이었다. 더 이상 나를 상대하지도 혼내지도 않는 세계가 너무나 괴물스

and blew them up using small rocks, inhaling the smoke to my content. With the last change in my pocket, I checked out adult comic books at my favorite comic book store on the street behind Bulranseo[5] Pharmacy where I sometimes got my father's Ativan prescription filled. I read them in the store, my eyes stinging with briquette fume, I thought a few times about the snowman that had most likely melted by now. As I was walking out of the store, having reread the last volume three times, I saw seasoned rice cakes cooking in saucepans on the charcoal heaters and was immediately filled with regret.

From there, I headed for the dark, drab streets of the Texas neighborhood[6] by Gireum Stream, which I had initially mistaken for Korean traditional dress shops. I bravely walked around enabled by my growling stomach and the pickle jar buried inside the snowman. Yet by the time I passed by the fried food places at the far end of the Texas neighborhood, I could barely stand the rich, delicious smell of the cheap cooking oil. Still, I didn't give in to the lure of the fried squid held out by the long-nailed hookers who couldn't make it home for the holidays. I had to hold onto my self-respect, if

럽고 슬퍼서 싱거운 눈물이라도 흘려야 직성이 풀릴 듯했다. 하긴 눈물 서너 방울쯤 짜내는 것은 일도 아니었으니까. 난 시래기 줄기가 매달린 처마 밑에 서서 몇 방울 떨구며 소리 없이 울었다. 차라리 그 깨진 단지라도 제자리를 지키고 있었다면 혼은 나더라도 나는 혼돈스럽지도 불안해하지도 않았을 것 아닌가.

"뭘 잘했다고 소리 없이 눈물을 꼭꼭 짜니? 정초부터 에밀 못 잡아먹어서 그러니? 넉살 좋게 단지를 깨뜨려 눈사람 속에 파묻을 생각은 어찌 했담."

엄마가 물에 젖은 손으로 내 볼따구니를 야무지게 잡아 비틀며 어이가 없다는 듯 픽 웃음을 지었다. 그 얼얼함이 내 균형감각을 바로잡아주었다. 아주머니들의 웃음소리 사이에서 나는 울음을 딱 그쳤다. 그리고는 어른처럼 땅을 쿵쾅거리며 뛰쳐나와 이 골목 저 골목을 헤집으며 어딘가를 향해 가슴이 터져라고 마구 달리고 또 달렸다. 그렇게 컸다.

"그래 딴 데는 안 들르고?"

"오다가 저기 전에 살던 기찻집이라고 있어요. 옛날 침례교회 밑에 말예요."

"으응, 있었지."

nothing else, so that I could endure the beatings and scoldings I would get later.

Before I knew it, the sun was setting. I returned to the nine-family house where by now my secret had surely been long exposed. I took a few deep breaths in front of the gate. I could only think about not wanting Mom to beat me with briquette tongs. But as I walked on the step-stone bridge across the ditch in front of the house, nobody paid any attention to me. When they should all have been surrounding me, consoling and pitying me, they acted instead as if nothing unusual had happened: strolling by with cooking pots, laughing with their hands over their mouths, talking congenially, and gathering by the common water faucet in the front yard to rinse rice. That included Mom, who was there cleaning up dried radish leaves. She saw me; but she didn't even give me any grief along the lines of "Where have you been? You missed lunch!" I was seriously baffled. They could have all been in on this together, to confuse me even more. I snuck a peek at the outhouse where I had oh-so-casually put up the snowman. There was nothing. The snowman had been completely wiped out. Of course, also nowhere to be seen

"거기 뭐 좀 볼 게 있어서 들어가려다 개조심이라고 쓰여 있어서 제대로 보지도 못하고 나왔어요. 보니깐 너무 바뀌었어요. 지붕도 기와에서 슬래브로 바뀌고 마당 쪽까지 집을 새로 지어서 반지하까지 치면 이층이나 다름없대요."

형이 고개를 건성으로 주억거렸다.

"형, 조합일 보면 보수는 좀 나와요?"

"돈?"

"예."

"정식으로 받는 급료는 한 푼도 없지. 하지만 나야 큰 돈은 못 만지지만 청탁이 큰 이권사업이 물렸으니 잘만 하면 떡고물깨나 묻힐 수 있는 자리지, 그 자리가. 근데 너 참 아버님 틀사진 가지러 왔다며 아랫집엔 안 들를 거니?"

"그만둘까봐요. 대낮부터 벌겋게 술도 마시고…… 또 불쑥 찾아간다는 게 좀 그렇잖아요. 돈 삼만 원 건네주는 건데 엄마가 말한 대로 온라인 이용하는 게 낫죠 뭐."

"그건 또 그래. 그럼 나랑 같이 마을버스 타고 내려갈래? 지하철 타려면. 아니면, 나랑 조합 사무실에 들러서 커피나 마시며 이곳 돌아가는 얘기나 좀 듣고 가든지."

was the pickle jar, whose hideous appearance should have been on full display. What on earth could have transpired?

The world surrounding me felt immensely unfamiliar. There was a yawning gap between the world of my speculation and thought, and the world in real life. That sense of distance stemmed from the realization that the world actually revolved without any respect to me, and the dawning realization that I was never at the center of anything. I almost needed to shed a couple of lame tears to get over the sadness of this monstrous world that could not be bothered to chastise, or even notice, me. Crying at the drop of a hat was nothing to me. I produced a few silent tears, standing under the eaves where radish leaves hung. If the broken jar had stayed put in its spot, I would not have been so confused or anxious, though I might have been punished anyway.

"Why are you crying like that, with what you have done? Are you hell-bent on killing your mother, within days of New Year's?" Mom asked. "And where on earth did you get the bold idea to break the jar and bury it like that in the snowman?"

Snorting from delighted incredulousness, Mom

"듣긴요 뭘. 형이 어련히 잘 알아서 해줄까."

"내가 해주긴 뭘. 네가 딱지를 팔고 싶다든지 아니면 그냥 입주를 하겠다든지 가부간에 결정을 내리면 내가 아무튼 최고 시세로 되도록 다리는 놔줄 순 있겠지. 내 생각엔 니가 어머니를 모시고 있으니까 당장 현찰이 필요한 게 아니라면 이리저리 굴려서 분양받을 때까지 기다렸다가 처분하는 게 장땡인데."

"예…… 엄마가 결정을 할 거예요. 전 심부름이나 몇 번 하면 되겠죠 뭐."

아무래도 마을버스 종점까지 가기는 그른 모양이었다. 거기까지 간다고 해서 변소가 어서옵쇼 하고 대령하고 있으라는 법도 없지 않은가. 나는 똥이 마려웠던 것이다. 아랫배가 이렇게 딱딱한 걸 보니 모르긴 몰라도 애들 팔뚝만한 걸로 한 자쯤은 뽑아낼 수 있을 듯했다.

"형 먼저 가세요. 전 다음에 또 올게요."

"왜? 버스 안 타?"

"예, 뭐가 갑자기 생각나서요."

나는 미주알에 힘을 잔뜩 주고는 형의 등을 떼밀어 마침 출발하려고 하는 마을버스 안으로 밀어넣었다. 그리고는 폐허 사이로 난 내리막길을 내달렸다. 반쯤 부

grinned and pinched my cheek, giving it a good twist. The tingling from the pinch restored my sense of balance. Surrounded by laughter from the women, I stopped my crying cold. Then, I stamped out of the house like an adult and kept running, my heart bursting, passing street after street to who knows where. That's how I grew up.

"So you're not dropping by anywhere else?" Chang asked me on our way to the bus depot.

"On the way here, there's this house called the train house, where I used to live. Near where the old Baptist church used to be, you know."

"I remember."

"I dropped by there to check something out but I couldn't even get a good look around because of the 'Beware of Dogs' sign. It's changed so much, though. The roof is no longer bricks but slab, and they added on to the house on the yard side, so including the half-basement, it's just like a two-story house now."

Chang nodded absentmindedly.

"Chang, do you get compensated by the association at all?"

"Money, you mean?"

"Yeah."

서진 집들이 몇 채 보이자 나는 그리로 뛰어들었다. 아무리 사람이 버리고 간 집이지만 똥 눌 곳이 마땅치 않았다. 얼마 전만 해도 밥 먹고 잠자던 부엌이나 방이라고 생각하니 선뜻 바지춤을 까내릴 수가 없었다.

잠시 주춤거리는 새에 마침 세로로 절반쯤 깨진 큼직한 항아리가 눈에 띄었다. 그 안에는 아마 그 항아리의 반을 깨고 들어왔을 한 뼘짜리 벽돌이 들어 있었다. 크기로 봐서는 한 열 명쯤 되는 식구는 좋이 먹여 살렸을 장독 같았다. 나는 누렇게 마른 소금기 자국이 얼비치는 옹색한 항아리 안으로 엉덩이를 비집고 들어가 벽돌과 깨진 장독 쪼가리를 디디고 서서 허리띠를 풀었다. 귀밑이 달아오르도록 용을 쓰느라 기침이 터졌다. 기침이 끝나자 나는 서러운 아이처럼 입초리가 비죽비죽 위로 치켜져 올라가는 걸 알았다. 울고 싶은 모양이었다. 나는 구린내가 나는 두 가랑이 사이로 고개를 바짝 쑤셔 박고 굵은 김이 무럭무럭 오르는 굵은 황금빛 똥을 쳐다보았다. 왠지 모르게 뿌듯했다.

그런데 나는 왜 구린내가 진동하는 깨진 항아리 속에서 똥을 누는 데 울고 싶어졌을까? 늙은 어머니와 아내 그리고 이제 막 초콜릿 맛을 안 네 살배기 아이, 이렇게

"Not a dime officially. But even though I won't see the big bucks, I could get my hands on a few good-sized crumbs if things fall into place, what with the concession industry involved that's into heavy lobbying. That's the kind of position I have there. By the way, you said you were getting your father's funeral photo and you're not stopping by the property down the hill?"

"I'd better not. I'm red and buzzed from drinking in the middle of the day and all." I trailed off a little. "Also, it's kind of not nice to show up just like that. It's only thirty thousand *won*, so it would be better to transfer it online like my mom said."

"Well, that is true. Then do you wanna take the shuttle down with me? To get to the subway? Or you could come with me to the association office and have coffee. They'll fill you in on what's going on in different parts of town."

"No need for that. I trust you to take special care of things for us."

"Oh, there's not much for me to do. If you want to sell the deed or just move in, whichever you decide to do, I could arrange for things so that you get the highest market price. I just think, since you're living with your mother, it would be best to hold

세 사람의 식솔을 거느린 가장이 비록 속눈썹이나마 이렇게 주책없이 적셔서야 되겠는가, 아아. 하지만 여태껏 나를 지탱해왔던 기억, 그 기억을 지탱해온 육체인 이 산동네가 사라진다는 것이 아니겠는가, 나를 이렇게 감상적으로 만드는 게. 이 동네가 포크레인의 날카로운 삽질에 깎여 가면 내 허약한 기억도 송두리째 퍼내어질 것이다. 그런데 나는 기껏 똥을 눌 뿐인데…… 그것 밖에 할 일이 없는데…….

똥을 다 누고 난 나는 빈집을 나와 모래주머니를 발목에서 풀어낸 달리기 선수처럼 가뿐하게 폐허 사이로 뚜벅뚜벅 걸어 들어갔다. 뒤를 돌아다보니 냄새를 맡은 누렁이 한 마리가 내가 나온 집으로 코를 쑤셔 박고 들어가는 모습이 보였다. 나는 입술을 굳게 다물었다. 그리고는 뭔가를 잃어버린 사람처럼 주위를 계속해서 두리번거리며 걷기 시작했다.

『신풍근 배커리 약사』, 문학동네, 2002

on to it until you're awarded a unit and then sell it, unless you need cash right away. Even if you have to deal with the tenants."

"Right… It'll be up to my mom anyway. I'll probably just have to run errands for her a couple of times."

I would not be able to make it to the shuttle bus stop at the depot. I realized it right there as my lower abdomen seized up. Even if I could make it, there wouldn't be a toilet waiting just for me there at the stop. The sensation in my lower abdomen was now rock-hard. I could probably push out a foot or so of stuff, thick as a child's forearm.

"You go on ahead. I'll come again soon."

"What, you're not getting on the bus?"

"Right, I just remembered something."

Tensing up my sphincter, I pushed Chang's back onto the departing shuttle bus. Then I ran down the path amidst the ruins. When I came to an area with a few half-destroyed houses, I dashed in. Although their occupants had abandoned them, it was difficult to find a suitable spot for taking a dump. I could not bring myself to lower my pants knowing that I was standing in a place where, until very recently, someone had slept, cooked and eaten.

While I agonized, my eyes spotted a large pot split lengthwise down the middle. Judging from its size, the jar must have been used to feed a family of ten or so easily. Inside the broken pot, there was a brick the size of my hand. Most likely it was what had broken it. Backing in butt-first to the cramped jar, stained yellow from dry salt, I positioned myself by stepping on the brick and broken pieces, and undid my belt. I broke out in coughs from pushing hard enough to get my body flushed all the way up to my earlobes. When the coughing subsided, I realized that my lips were curled up at the ends like those of a child in sorrow. Apparently, I felt like crying. I tucked my head tight in between my thighs close to the foul stink. I looked at the shit, thick and golden with warm, thick steam rising from it. For some reason, I felt gratified.

But why did I feel like crying while shitting in a broken jar swirling with a foul stink? How could the head of a household of four, with an old mother, a wife, and a four-year-old toddler, who had just discovered chocolate, get wet around his eyes, so undignifiedly, even if it was only his eyelashes that got wet? Ah. Still, we were talking about the imminent disappearance of this slummy town in the hills, the physical body that had sustained my memory, which in turn had sustained me. That is what was making me sentimental. As the excavators carved up the town, they would also gouge out my frail memories of this place. But I was only taking a dump here... there was nothing else I could do...

When I was done, I left the empty house and walked right into the middle of the ruins. I felt as light as a runner after removing sand weights from his ankles. I looked back to see a mutt going nose-first into the house I had just left, trailing after the smell. I pursed my lips. Then, like a man who's lost something, I started to walk, looking steadily around me.

1) *Uwagi*, a Japanese word meaning "jacket," was used by some Koreans in the 20th century.
2) *Pparu* is the Korean rendering of the Japanese バール, from the English "crowbar," and is still used by some in construction.
3) Carbonated energy drink.
4) Korean transliteration of the Japanese セメント (cement).
5) Sino-Koreanized pronunciation of "France."
6) A Korean slang for a red light district.

Translated by Chris Choi

해설

Afterword

기억을 통한 현실 재현

이경재 (문학평론가)

서른다섯의 나이로 요절한 김소진은 칠 년여의 기간 동안 네 권의 소설집과 두 권의 장편소설을 펴냈다. 김소진의 작품은 그야말로 서민들의 삶을 관념이 아닌 날것 그대로 드러내었다. 이러한 삶의 구체성 이면에 자리 잡은 지식인으로서의 복잡한 자의식은 그의 문학을 한층 풍요롭게 만들어준다. 서민들의 삶에 대한 실감나는 리얼리티는 가난한 미아리 산동네에서 유년기와 청년기를 보낸 김소진의 이력과 밀접한 관련이 있다. 김소진의 문학은 개발기 서울 산동네에 자리를 틀고 간신히 버텨 나갔던 수많은 서민들에 대한 정밀한 기록화라고 보아도 무리가 없다. 김소진 소설에서 핍진하게 재

Reality Reenacted Through Memory

Lee Kyung-jae (literary critic)

Kim So-jin's life was cut short at 33, but in only seven years' time he managed to produce four volumes of short stories and two novels. Throughout all of his works, Kim portrayed the lives of common people as they were rather than as abstractions. What gave his works their richness was their complex self-consciousness within the realm of gritty, ordinary human life.

This naturalistic realism in Kim's work is closely related to Kim's own life history. He spent his boyhood and young adulthood in a poor neighborhood in the hills of Miari, Seoul. Thus, it would not be preposterous to consider Kim's work a meticu-

현된 서민들의 삶은 전통적인 리얼리즘 소설과는 달리 기억을 통과한 것이라는 점에서 그 독특성이 있다. 이처럼 기억을 통한 재현이라는 고유한 양상은 자연스럽게 김소진의 작품이 메타소설로서의 성격을 지니게 만든다. 김소진의 마지막 발표작이 된 「눈사람 속의 검은 항아리」는 기억으로서의 현실 재현이 지닌 의미와 한계, 그리고 김소진이 맞닥뜨렸던 작가로서의 자의식을 예리하게 보여준 명작이다.

「눈사람 속의 검은 항아리」는 선명한 이분법으로 이루어진 세계이다. 이분법을 성립시키는 대타항으로는 '눈사람이 된 항아리/똥통이 된 항아리' '피로/가뿐함' '상상의 세계/실재의 세계' '산동네/재개발' 등이 있다. 작가 김소진이라고 보아 무리가 없는 소설 속 민홍은 들뜬 기대감을 가지고 미아리 셋집에 다녀오려 한다. 재개발을 앞둔 동네 사정도 파악하고 아버지 영정 사진도 가져오겠다는 것이 어머니에게 말하는 표면적인 이유이다. 그러나 미아리 셋집을 다시 찾는 진정한 이유는 "그 종이처럼 얇은 기억이 나를 이렇게 사라져가려는 동네로 밀고 가는 것이 아닐까?"라는 말에서 알 수 있듯이, 지난날의 '기억' 때문이다. 김소진의 작품 세계를 지탱

lous record of the countless common people who settled in this hilly Seoul neighborhood during its developmental period and barely managed to get by. Singular to Kim's writing, then, and unlike other more traditional works of realism, is the manner in which he reenacts of the lives of the ordinary characters in true-to-life form, a product achieved through Kim's own memory. This unique aspect of reenacting reality through memory naturally gives his works the characteristics of a meta-fiction. "The Dark Jar within the Snowman," Kim's last published work, is one such exceptional metafictional piece that acutely shows the significance and the limits of reenacting reality as memory, as well as an authorial self-consciousness with which Kim had to constantly contend.

The world of "The Dark Jar within the Snowman" is one made up of a clear dichotomies. The dichotomies in Kim's story include "the jar that turned into the snowman/ the jar that turned into a poop receptacle," "fatigue/ lightness," "the imagined world/ the real world," and "the hilly neighborhood/ the redevelopment area." In "The Dark Jar Within the Snowman," the character Min-hong, whom we can reasonably take to be the author

하는 기반이 미아리 산동네였다는 것을 고려할 때, 이 곳을 둘러보는 작업은 곧바로 자신의 지난 작가 세계를 되돌아보는 일로 연결된다.

그 '기억'은 한 지붕 아홉 가구의 장석조네 집에서 있었던 20년 전 어느 겨울날의 일이다. 갑자기 오줌이 마려워 한밤중에 화장실을 다녀오던 민홍은 빠루를 잘못 밟아 짠지가 담긴 함경도 욕쟁이 할머니네 항아리를 깨뜨린다. 평소에 어머니는 정초에 물건이 깨지거나 금이 가는 것에 대하여 심각한 금기를 지니고 있었기에 민홍의 걱정은 더욱 커진다. 그 순간 민홍은 밤새 내린 눈으로 항아리를 덮어 씌운 눈사람을 만들어 감추고는 하루 동안의 가출을 감행한다. 이 일을 거치며 어린 민홍은 박탄-D 병을 쥐어짜서 나온 액체로는 도저히 풀 수 없는 엄청난 피로감을 느낀다. 이 대목에서는 반복적으로 피로라는 단어가 연이어 등장한다.

가출한 날 저녁 어린 민홍은 엄마에게 엄청난 야단을 맞게 될 거라고 걱정하며 집으로 돌아오지만, 눈사람이 있던 자리는 이미 깨끗하게 치워져 있다. 더욱 놀라운 사실은 민홍을 야단치는 사람은 고사하고 신경 쓰는 사람조차 없다는 사실이다. 이 순간 민홍은 "내가 짐작하

himself, sets out noticeably excited to visit the rental property in Miari. The explicit purpose of the trip is to get a sense of the soon-to-be redeveloped neighborhood as well as to bring back a memorial photograph of his father. But the true reason for his return to the rental property in Miari is —as can be gleaned from "Could it be that the paper-thin memory was now pushing me toward the town soon to disappear?"—is the memory of the yesterdays. Considering the foundation of Kim's literary world was that neighborhood in the hills of Miari, the task of surveying this area is directly connected to his own remembrances as a writer.

The memory that so haunts Min-hong is about what happened on a winter day twenty years ago at Jang Seok-jo's heavily populated house. On his way back from the outhouse—after getting an urge to urinate in the middle of the night—Min-hong steps on a "*pparu*" and breaks a pickle jar belonging to the old lady from Hamgyeong Province with a penchant for swearing. His anxiety is magnified due to his mother's taboo of breaking or cracking things during the New Year. On the spot, Min-hong makes a snowman out of the snow that has fallen overnight to conceal the broken jar and runs

고 또 생각하는 세계하고 실제 세계 사이에는 이렇듯 머나먼 거리가 놓여 있었던 것"임을 절감한다. 20년이 지난 민홍이 이 기억에 그토록 집착하는 것은, 현재의 그 역시 실재와 상상 사이의 간극으로 고민하기 때문이다. 실제로 민홍은 미아리를 다시 찾아가지만, 그곳은 민홍이 기억하던(달리 말하자면 김소진이 목숨을 걸고 소설 속에서 형상화하던) 미아리와는 매우 다르다. "보니깐 너무 바뀌었어요."라는 민홍의 말처럼, 사람도 건물도 모든 것이 변해 있다. 재개발 경기의 훈풍으로 이미 미아리 사람들의 얼굴에 궁기는 사라지고 없다. 그들은 물질적으로는 가난할지언정 인간으로서의 품격은 잃지 않던 과거의 서민들이 더 이상 아니다. 소설에서 반복적으로 강조되는 그들의 육식성은 변모된 이들의 모습을 드러내기에 모자람이 없다. 민홍이 좋아하던 창이형은 부도덕한 행실로 마을 사람 모두로부터 손가락질 받던 국희와 살림을 차리고 있다. 이러한 상황에서 셋집에 들르지 않고 집으로 돌아오던 민홍은 세로로 절반쯤 깨진 큼직한 항아리에 대변을 본다. 똥을 다 눈 후에 민홍은 "모래주머니를 발목에서 풀어낸 달리기 선수처럼 가뿐하게" 걷기 시작한다.

away for the day. Throughout this ordeal, the narrator begins to feel a kind of heavy fatigue that cannot be alleviated by any of his efforts. In this part of the story, the word "fatigue" appears repeatedly.

After he has spent the whole day outside of the house, the young Min-hong returns home worried about being severely punished by his mother. However, he comes home only to find a clean, empty spot where the snowman once was. Even more surprising is the fact that, not only is no one yelling at him, but not a single person seems to be even paying any attention to him at all. It is at that moment that he realizes that there was "such a big distance between the world of my speculation and thought, and that in real life."

The reason Min-hong is so obsessed with this memory after twenty years is that in the present he still agonizes over the distance between the real and the imagined. When Min-hong actually does return to Miari, the place is decidedly different from the Miari of his memory, and, by extension, the Miari to which Kim So-jin risked his life to give form to in his stories. Everything, including people and buildings, has changed as Min-hong says: "(i)t's

이십 년 전 민홍이 깨진 항아리에 눈을 씌워 예쁜 눈사람을 만들었다면, 20년이 지난 민홍은 깨진 항아리 안에 똥을 싼다. 민홍이 어린 시절 항아리를 깨뜨림으로써 실재와 상상의 격차를 느꼈다면, 이십 년이 지난 민홍은 미아리를 방문하여 다시 한 번 실재와 상상의 격차를 확인하고 있다. 김소진에게 미아리란 '깨진' 항아리처럼, 그를 작가로서 살게 한 가장 근원적인 외상의 지점이라고 할 수 있다. 그것을 애써 눈으로 감춰 그럴듯한 눈사람을 만드는 것이야말로 김소진 문학에 대한 가장 명징한 표상이다. 이 눈사람을 만드는 작업이 필사적인 만큼 그 피로감 역시도 치명적이었던 것이다. 그것은 어린 민홍이 항아리를 깨뜨렸던 그날 밤에 느꼈던 그 엄청난 피로감을 통해 유추할 수 있다. 이십 년 전 어린 민홍이 느끼던 피로 역시도 현재의 민홍이 떠올린 것이기 때문이다. 민홍은 미아리 산동네를 떠나며 더 이상 그 피로를 감당하지 않으려 한다. 민홍이 작품의 마지막에 울면서 하는 "여태껏 나를 지탱해왔던 기억, 그 기억을 지탱해온 육체인 이 산동네가 사라진다는 것이 아니겠는가"라는 생각에서 알 수 있듯이, 이제는 깨진 항아리마저 존재하지 않기 때문이다. 이러한 절체절

changed so much." The warm wind of the redevelopment-aided market has already erased the traces of want from the faces of the Miari people. They are no longer the common folk who kept their dignity intact in the midst of abject poverty. Their carnivorousness, repeatedly emphasized in the story, is enough to reveal this change. Additionally, Chang, the older boy Min-hong used to look up to, is now shacking up with Guk-hee, a former target of ridicule in the village for her promiscuous behavior. Given these changes, Min-hong, on his way back and without even dropping by the rental property, defecates into a large, vertically broken jar. After he finishes, Min-hong starts to walk "as light as a runner after taking off sand weights from his ankles."

While the Min-hong of twenty years ago put snow over one broken jar to make a snowman, twenty years later he defecates into another broken jar. The young Min-hong senses the distance between the real and the imagined by breaking the jar, and twenty years later he reconfirms the distance between these two poles when he visits Miari. Along with the broken jar, Miari could be considered the location of the fundamental trauma

명의 상황에서 민홍은 깨진 항아리에 똥을 누는 나름의 결별의식을 행한다. 이 상처와의 결별이 바로 민홍이 느끼는 '가뿐함'의 근원이었던 것이다. 자신의 소설에 대한 자의식으로 가득찬 「눈사람 속의 검은 항아리」는 김소진이 이전의 자기 세계와는 다른 새로운 문학적 지평을 향해 나아가고 있었음을 선명하게 보여준다.

most responsible for Kim's life as a writer. The act of covering it over so painstakingly with snow to make a respectable snowman is the most lucid symbol in Kim's works.

As desperate as the labor to make the snowman can be, this sense of fatigue it causes is just as fatal. It can be inferred from the massive sense of fatigue Min-hong feels on the night he breaks the jar. After all, that fatigue felt by the young Min-hong twenty years before, is also what the adult Min-hong recalls in the present. As he leaves the hilly neighborhood of Miari, Min-hong tries not to burden himself with this feeling any longer. This is because now, as Min-hong's tearful comment attests at the end, "still, we were talking about the imminent disappearance of this slummy town in the hills, the physical body that had sustained my memory, which in turn had sustained me." Even the broken jar is no longer there.

In this absolutely dire moment, Min-hong's choice of a farewell ceremony is to defecate into another broken jar. This wounded parting was the very origin of the "lightness" Min-hong feels. Filled with a self-consciousness in his own fiction, "The Dark Jar within the Snowman" vividly illustrates Kim

So-jin's evolution towards a literary form entirely different from the kinds of writings he—and many writers—have created before.

비평의 목소리

Critical Acclaim

김소진의 소설 세계는 크게 세 가지 계열로 나눠진다. (가)가 월남한 아비와 관련된 부자간의 관계이자 그에 멈추지 않는 분단 이데올로기의 간접화라는 점에서, (나)가 지식인의 역사의식의 노출이라는 점에서, 그리고 (다)가 미아리 길음 천변 달동네의 사람들, 이른바 '장석조네 사람들'의 삶을 다루었다는 점에서 각각 주목되었다. (가)는 개인의 집안 사정이지만, 그것이 그대로 분단 이데올로기에 걸려 있는 만큼, 이 나라 소설 주류에 이어진 것이었으며, 구소련이 해체되었다고는 하나 아직도 여전히 거세게 소용돌이치는 인류사의 미래에 대한 관심사가 그림자를 드리우고 있는 과제가 (나)였

The world of Kim So-jin's fiction can be divided into three main types, each of which drew critical attention: Type A: fiction that dealt with father-son relationships pertaining to fathers who were refugees from the North, as well as fiction that went a step further to deal indirectly with the ideology of division; Type B: fiction that revealed the historical awareness of the intellectual. And Type C: fiction that tackled the lives of the residents from the slums by the Miari Gireum stream, the so-called "people at Jang Seok-jo's." While Type A had to do with the circumstances of one's family, they came from the ideology of division and so were con-

기에 그만큼 현실적이었고, 영원한 고향인 민중의 삶의 터전인 달동네 얘기인 (다)는 원초적인 자리였던 것이다. 이 세 가지 과제를 동시에 전개하고 있는 신인 김소진의 존재가 돋보였음은 어디까지나 그 잠재력이랄까 가능성의 차원에서였던 것이다.

김윤식

김소진의 소설은 '사이'(in-between)의 소설이다. 돌아보자. 투박하고 리얼한 밑바닥 민중의 삶과 언어를 소설의 중핵으로 끌어안았다는 점에서 우리는 얼핏 그의 소설에 드리워진 '80년대'를 보았고, 그럼에도 불구하고 관념성이라는 불가피한 폐해와 거리가 멀었다는 점에서 그것과의 의미 있는 단절을 보았다. 또 한편 그의 소설에서 섬세한 개인의 내면과 허무주의의 기미를 엿본 이는 그것을 근거로 그의 소설을 비루한 개인의 욕망과 상처의 아우라로 꽃핀 저 '90년대'의 징후로 편입시키고픈 유혹도 있었겠지만, 내면에 달라붙어 웅성대는 밑바닥 타자의 목소리들은 그 유혹을 지긋이 거절하는 것이기도 했다. 그의 소설은 영락없는 지식인적 자의식을 수줍게 달고 있으면서도 달동네와 주변부 하류 인생들

nected to this country's mainstream fictional traditions; Type B was rooted in realism, grappling with the issues of the direction history would take even after the dissolution of the USSR and the collapse of the Soviet bloc. Finally, Type C had to do with the primodial stories, stories of a hilly slum as the eternal hometown, serving as the base of living for the people. The presence of the newcomer Kim So-jin, who moved along these three pursuits simultaneously, stood out for his potential and possibilities as a writer.

Kim Yun-sik

Kim So-jin's stories are stories of the "in-between." Let us look back. We saw how the "1980s" shaded his fiction, which embraced the lives and language of unpolished, real folks as their nucleus. Yet, we also saw his writing make a meaningful severance from that era, distancing itself from the unavoidable evil of ideality. On the other hand, those who sensed from his fiction a delicate interiority of individuals and nihilism might be tempted to classify them as products of the "1990s," when the aura of individuals' desires and wounds flourished. But the insistent voices of individuals from

의 누추하고 비루한 삶과 함께하며 빛나고 있었다. 김소진 소설의 개성은 기억과 현실, 환각과 일상, '날것'과 관념, 지식인과 '양아치'의 사이에서 그 양편의 감각이 뒤섞이면서 만들어내는 특이한 그 어떤 것이라고도 할 수 있겠다. 김소진의 소설은 그렇게 모든 '이것'과 '저것'의 사이에서 그 둘과 관계하면서도 바로 그것을 통해 그 모두를 거리화하고 반성하는 소설이었다.

김영찬

김소진의 작품은 그간 여타 작가들의 후일담 소설에서 이념의 과잉과 상실의 시대로 인식되던, 그리하여 다소 윤리적 시각에서 바라보던 80년대와 90년대를 민중적 삶이 지탱해온 우리 역사의 한 부분으로 포섭하였다. 아버지와 어머니, 장석조네 사람들로 대표되는 서민대중들의 '쑥부쟁이' 같은 삶, 그러나 그 속에서 피어나는 '달개비꽃' 같은 희망이 그를, 그의 문학을 키운 토양이었다. 그의 소설에는 '그들'의 삶의 애환이 담긴 언어가 유려하게 펼쳐져 있다. 뿐만 아니라 '그들'의 과거는 80년대, 90년대의 '그'의 삶과 그물처럼 엮이고 서로 매개되어서 '지금 이 순간'과 '과거'는 역사의 커다란 물

the bottom, those clinging to the interior, gave a refined refutation to that temptation. While his stories were sheepishly in possession of an unmistakable intellectual self-consciousness, Kim's stories shone (and shone the brightest) when they were in the hilly slums and surrounded by the squalid and abject existences of those living in them. The distinctive quality of his fiction can be attributed to the mixing of contrary senses: memory and reality, the fantastic and the mundane, the "raw" and the ideal, and the intellectual and the "louse." Thus, Kim's fiction related to two opposite sides, between every pair of "this" and "that," and, through this relationship to the pairs, both distanced and absolved them.

Kim Yeong-chan

Kim So-jin's works subsumed the part of Korean history sustained by the lives of the people from the 1980s and 1990s, eras that we now consider ones of excess and ideology loss, eras that are now consequently regarded from a somewhat ethical vantage point in other writers' stories of remembrance. The lives of common folk, represented by his father, mother, and the other families at

줄기로 이어져 있다. 김소진은 우리 당대를 고민스럽게 살아가는 자들의 본질을 이념적 차원에서가 아니라 구체적 역사의 차원에서 복원해 놓은 90년대 최초의 작가이다.

서경석

Jang Seok-jo's house, persevered like an "aster" in Kim's writing. They were the hope that bloomed like "dayflowers" and were the soil from which he, and his literary works, grew. His fictions gracefully displayed the language that conveyed the joys and sorrows from their lives. Furthermore, their past and his life during the 1980s and the 1990s are interwoven and act as each other's intermediary counterparts, leading to a single great historical current connecting the here-and-now and the past. Kim So-jin is the first writer of the 1990s who restored the essence of those who led agonized existences in the present era, not through ideological dimensions, but through specifically historical ones.

Seo Kyeong-seok

김소진

1963년 강원도 철원에서 아버지 김응수 어머니 김영혜의 이남이녀 중 막내로 태어났다. 함경남도 성진이 고향인 아버지는 원산 대철수 때 처자식을 포화 속에 남기고 혼자 월남하였다. 1967년 군수품 장사가 어려워지자 서울로 이사와 미아리 산동네에 자리 잡는다. 1968년 아버지가 중풍으로 쓰러진 이후 어머니가 삯바느질 등으로 생계를 떠맡는다. 1982년 서울대학교 인문대에 입학하고, 2학년 때 영문과를 선택한다. 대학 시절 집회와 시위에 열심히 참여했지만, 어느 때부터 거리에서 싸우는 데 자신감을 잃으면서 차선책으로 황석영, 이문구, 박완서의 작품들을 대상으로 소설 습작에 몰두했다. 1984년 서울대 영문과 학회지 《생성》에 소설 「아버지의 슈퍼마켓」「소외」와 시 「조명」을 발표한다. 1986년부터 1년 반 동안 방위 생활을 하며 우리말 어휘, 어구, 속담 등을 대학노트에 기록하며 정리한다. 이때 습득한 어휘와 자라면서 어머니 곁에서 들어야 했던 입심이 합쳐져 소설 문체의 중요한 밑거름이 형성된다.

Kim So-jin

Kim So-jin was born in Cheorwon, Gangwon-do in 1963, the youngest child of Kim Ung-su and Kim Yeong-hye, who had another son and two daughters in addition to Kim. Originally from Seongjin in the Hamgyeongnam-do his father moved south by himself, leaving his first wife and their children during the retreat of Wonsan during the Korean War. When his father's military supplies business ran into financial trouble in 1967, the family moved to Seoul, settling in the slums in the hills of Miari. After his father's incapacitation following a stroke, his mother became the sole breadwinner of the family, working as a seamstress among other things. Kim entered the School of Humanities at Seoul National University in 1982, and as a sophomore decided to major in English. A zealous participant in political meetings and protests throughout college, as his confidence in street-protest waned he later chose to concentrate on fiction writing, training with the works of Hwang Sok-yong, Yi Mun-gu, and Park Wan-seo. Shortly after-

1991년「쥐잡기」가 경향신문 신춘문예에 당선되어 등단한다. 1993년 김윤식 선생의 주례로 소설가 함정임과 결혼하고, 이듬해 아들 태형이 태어난다. 1996년 문화의 날에 문화체육관광부가 수여하는 제4회 오늘의 젊은 예술가상을 수상하고, 계간《한국문학》편집위원으로 참여한다. 1997년 4월 22일 새벽에 별세한다.

wards, his short stories, "Father's Store" and "Alienation," and his poem, "Spotlight," were published in the English Departmental journal, *Saengseong* (Creation) in 1984. While he was completing his military service in the Korean National Guard, Kim, for a year and a half starting from 1986, recorded and organized Korean vocabulary, phrases, and proverbs in his college notebooks. The vocabulary he acquired during this time, combined with his mother's colorful speech patterns he'd endured growing up, became the foundation for his fiction writing style. He debuted as a professional writer when his story, "Mouse-Catching," won the *Kyunghyang Shinmun*'s annual spring literary contest in 1991. He married novelist Ham Jeong-im in 1993 at a wedding officiated by Kim Yun-sik. His son, Taehyeong, was born the following year. In 1996, he was awarded the fourth annual "Contemporary Young Artist Award" given by the Ministry of Culture, Sports and Tourism on Culture Day, and joined the quarterly journal *Hanguk Munhak* (Korean Literature) as an editor. He died in the early morning of April 22nd, 1997.

번역 **크리스 최** Translated by Chris Choi

인문학자, 문화언어 컨설턴트. 매사추세츠 공대와 하버드에서 비교문학 박사 포함 총 네 개의 학위를 받았으며, 현재 뉴욕에 있는 컨설팅 펌 Educhora와 비영리단체인 Educhora Culture의 디렉터이다.

Chris Choi is apparently into balance. Bicultural and bilingual, she earned two degrees from M.I.T., then two more at Harvard, her final one a doctorate in Comparative Literature. As Director of Educhora, she researches, consults and facilitates learning on linguistic and cultural interaction, transition, fluency and impact. In addition to also directing the non-profit Educhora Culture, she spends time enjoying sports and fashion.

감수 **데이비드 윌리엄 홍** Edited by David William Hong

데이비드 윌리엄 홍은 미국 일리노이주 시카고에서 태어났다. 일리노이대학교에서 영문학을, 뉴욕대학교에서 영어교육을 공부했다. 지난 2년간 서울에 거주하면서 처음으로 한국인과 아시아계 미국인 문학에 깊이 몰두할 기회를 가졌다. 현재 뉴욕에서 거주하며 강의와 저술 활동을 한다.

David William Hong was born in 1986 in Chicago, Illinois. He studied English Literature at the University of Illinois and English Education at New York University. For the past two years, he lived in Seoul, South Korea, where he was able to immerse himself in Korean and Asian-American literature for the first time. Currently, he lives in New York City, teaching and writing.

바이링궐 에디션 한국 대표 소설 031
눈사람 속의 검은 항아리

2013년 10월 18일 초판 1쇄 인쇄
2020년 4월 6일 초판 2쇄 발행

지은이 김소진 | **옮긴이** 크리스 최 | **펴낸이** 김재범
감수 데이비드 윌리엄 홍 | **기획** 정은경, 전성태, 이경재
편집 강민영, 김지연 | **관리** 박수연, 홍희표 | **디자인** 이춘희
펴낸곳 아시아 | **출판등록** 2006년 1월 31일 제319-2006-4호
주소 서울특별시 동작구 흑석동 100-16
전화 02.821.5055 | **팩스** 02.821.5057 | **홈페이지** www.bookasia.org
ISBN 978-89-94006-94-9 (set) | 978-89-94006-95-6 (04810)
값은 뒤표지에 있습니다.

Bi-lingual Edition Modern Korean Literature 031
The Dark Jar within the Snowman

Written by Kim So-jin | **Translated by** Chris Choi
Published by Asia Publishers | 100-16 Heukseok-dong, Dongjak-gu, Seoul, Korea
Homepage Address www.bookasia.org | **Tel**. (822).821.5055 | **Fax**. (822).821.5057
First published in Korea by Asia Publishers 2013
ISBN 978-89-94006-94-9 (set) | 978-89-94006-95-6 (04810)